THE MAN
WHO GREW
YOUNGER

THE MAN
WHO GREW
YOUNGER

and Other Stories

JEROME CHARYN

HARPER & ROW, PUBLISHERS
New York, Evanston, and London

*This book is for Harvey and Fannie
and Sam and Lippy and Misha.
And Marlene.*

CONTENTS

When the voices of children are heard on the green
And whisp'rings are in the dale,
The days of my youth rise fresh in my mind,
My face turns green and pale.

Then come home, my children, the sun is gone down,
And the dews of night arise;
Your spring & your day are wasted in play,
And your winter and night in disguise.

—WILLIAM BLAKE

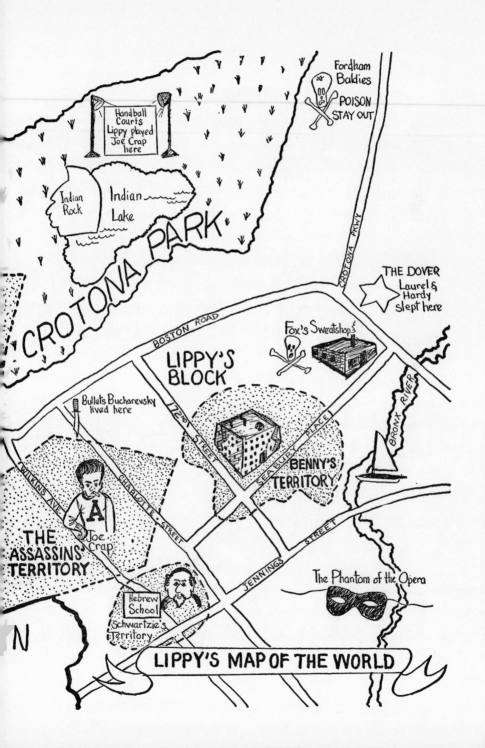

1944

So Pinocchio and Lamp-Wick and the hundred bad boys waited for the wagon to take them to the Land of Toys. Pinoke was a little nervous because he promised the Good Fairy he'd be home before dark and do his Hebrew homework and here it was with the moon already out. But Lamp-Wick called him a schmuck for worrying so much. That's what it says in the book! And the hundred boys kept whistling and shouting, "No more school! Hurray for the Land of Toys!" I was gonna pass the book over to Lippy when I read that, but he was too busy drawing a funny picture of Schwartzfarb, and I never like to bother him when he's doing his art work. So I just kept reading. Lamp-Wick told everybody that in the Land of Toys there was no school or nothin, just ice cream cones and charlotte russes and kosher pickles and all kinds of fun. Wait'll Lippy reads this! Then I hadda turn the page and that's when Schwartzie called on me. We were supposed to be reading the story about Abraham and the idols, and I always have the right answers, so that's why Schwartzie picked me. But this time I didn't know the answer, because I was trying to figure out what was gonna happen to Pinoke. Schwartzie touched the top of his yamulka and Lippy stopped drawing for a minute and gave him the voodoo sign. Seymour Pinkowitz made a coupla farts with his lip and that always cracks everybody up. Then Schwartzie started cursing me out. "Benny," he said, "you wanna wind up like your brother Leo over there, huh? A dunce, a *fershtupte kop!*" Lippy don't like it too much when anybody calls him Leo, so he put his hand under the desk and made another voodoo sign. But Schwartzie kept it up. "You wanna be the schlemiel number-two? . . . How will it look, a Jewish boy without a bar mitzvah, a *shandeh!*" Leo is two years older than me, but we're in the same Hebrew class. That's because he never does any work. Everybody knows he's never gonna get bar mitzvahed, because he's a terrible cut-up, and he don't even know two words in Hebrew. "*Oysgevarfeneh gelt!*" Schwartzie said, looking back and forth at Lippy and me. And I'm the smartest kid in the class!

Then Seymour Pinkowitz puffed out his cheeks and slapped them hard with his hands and he made the loudest lip fart I ever heard in my life. All the kids in the first row started holding their noses and calling Seymour a stink pot,

and I knew there was gonna be trouble, because Schwartzie
went looking for his stick. *"Banditen,"* he kept saying to himself. Seymour Pinkowitz was dying to make another lip fart,
but Lippy wouldn't give him the signal. Well, it's a lucky
thing that Schwartzie got some kinda trouble with his stomach, and it bothers him sometimes when he gets all excited,
or who knows what woulda happened. The way he was holding on to that stick, it looked like some heads were gonna
start flying for sure! But then he grabbed ahold of his
stomach and he hadda drop the stick. "Cancers I'm getting
from you, cancers." He started breathing out hard and in
between his breathing he let out a coupla "oy, oy, oys!"
Lippy got some water in a paper cup from the sink in the
toilet and brought it over to Schwartzfarb. Seymour said
Lippy shoulda pissed in the cup or something, but Lippy
wouldn't do nothin mean like that, especially when
Schwartzie is sick. Lippy don't take advantage of people. Not
that way! Schwartzie took the water, but Lippy hadda hold
his hand while he was drinking, it was shaking so much.
And some of the water spilled on his suit.

"Leo," Schwartzie said, so low that nobody but Lippy and
me could hear him, "tell everybody to go home!" All the kids
were making so much noise that Schwartzie put his hands
over his ears and said, *"Gevalt, gevalt!"* I could see he was in
a bad way. Then Lippy put two fingers in his mouth and he
made a whistle that was ten times louder than Seymour
Pinkowitz's loudest lip fart. And right away everybody shut
up. "Go home," Lippy said, just like that, and everybody
scrammed. Then he said to Schwartzie, "You want me to
stay with you, *Rebbe?*" Schwartzie's only a plain Hebrew

teacher, but he likes it when anybody calls him "Rebbe."
And Lippy knows it. Lippy can be a son-of-a-bitch, but he
knows how to be nice too. So I figured I'd follow up with a
coupla "Rebbes" of my own, and I said, "You want me to
erase the boards, Rebbe? Should I put the chalk back in the
box, huh, Rebbe, huh?" But when I said it, it sounded stupid.
I aint got Lippy's style. I think Lippy likes Schwartzfarb a
little, and if you ask me, Schwartzie likes him too. But he
can't show it in class, because of the way Lippy cuts up all
the time. But Schwartzfarb's okay. My mother pays him only
four dollars a month for Lippy and me, because my father's
dead, and believe it or not, the regular price is ten! Anyway,
Lippy got him another cupa water and I erased all the
blackboards, and then Schwartzie said we could go. "I'll be
all right, Leo, thanks. Go. Tell your mother she shouldn't
make me kishgah this week. . . . It's delicious, Leo, but
maybe it's no good for my stomach. You'll tell her, Leo?"

"Yeah. Benny'll tell her."

"Goodbye, boys. . . . And Leo, stay out of trouble, Leo.
You know how hard your mother works. She has enough
tzuris without you. . . ."

Lippy don't like it when anybody preaches to him, but he
didn't say nothin this time. He just said, "Yeah, yeah," and
then he touched my shoulder and we both left. On the way
down the stairs Lippy said to me, "I gotta go somewhere,
Benny. Tell Mommy not to worry. I'll be home late."

"Where ya gotta go, Lippy?"

"Stop asking me questions. I gotta go, that's all!"

I knew it wouldn't do me no good, but I said it anyway.
"Can I go with you, huh Lippy? I won't say nothin to
nobody, Lippy, I swear. . . ."

"What are ya, my pal all of a sudden? You know I never take nobody with me, so stop asking. I'm in a hurry."

"Lippy, where should I say you went, if Mommy wants to know?"

"Say I went looking for frogs."

"There's no frogs in the winter, Lippy."

"So say anything. You got a brain. Think!"

And then we got to the bottom of the stairs, and Lippy ran across the street. I saw him go toward Wilkins Avenue. I hoped he wouldn't get in trouble. But you don't hafta worry about Lippy. He can take care of himself. Hymie Moskowitz was waiting outside for me. We always go home together from Hebrew school. And Hymie said, "Ya wanna play marbles?"

"I can't, Hymie. I only got my puries on me. I didn't bring my shooter."

"That's okay. I got my puries too."

So me and Hymie started shooting immies in the street. We even forgot to take our yamulkas off. Hymie was winning all my puries and he kept dropping them in the old Band-Aid box that he saves special for puries. It was hard for me to aim because I had to hold my Hebrew books and shoot at the same time. Hymie wouldn't hold my books or nothin. He wasn't gonna give me a chance to win. Hymie aint no dope! I'm terrific when I got both hands free! Anyway, he said I should put my books down on the curb like he did. I wouldn't do that for a coupla lousy puries, it's a sin! Hymie knew it too, but he didn't give a damn. He wasn't gonna let anything like that spoil his game. Well, I was getting tired of giving up all my puries, so I put my jacket on the ground and then put my books on top of the jacket. It's all right that way, just so the books don't touch the ground. Schwartzie says that when you put your Hebrew books on the floor, especially your *siddur,* it's like slapping God right in the face. And everytime you drop them you gotta kiss them and everything. Everybody knows that! When Hymie saw me put down the books he closed his Band-Aid box. But he can't pull a stunt like that on me. I made him open up his box and take out five or six of his best puries. Then I set myself up for a perfect shot. My immie was about two spans away from his purie, so I breathed out hard and squatted down, and then Hymie picked up his purie and said, "Oh, oh, the Ass-ass-ins!" I looked up and saw Joe Crapanzano and three of his stooges from Freeman Street with their skull-and-crossbones jackets. Hymie had a little more sense then me. He hid his yamulka and kicked his Hebrew books away from the curb. One of Crapanzano's stooges stepped all over my Hebrew books and swiped Hymie's Band-Aid box with all the puries inside and I prayed that Hymie wouldn't cry because the Assassins hate sissies. But it was all right. Hymie didn't cry. He was too scared. He just sniffled a little. Then the stooge took the yamulka off my head and put it near his crotch and made out that it was a pissing cup or something and he turned it inside out and held it with two fingers and let it drop like it was some kind of a parachute. I didn't say nothin because I knew God could strike him down dead on the spot for doing such a thing if He wanted to. But God don't pay much attention to the goys. He's only extra hard on the Jews. Anyway, the stooge looked at me and said, "Who gave ya permission to play here, huh Jew boy?"

Then stooge number two said, "Leave him alone, Lefty. You know who he is, huh? That's Lippy's kid brother!"

I knew it would come out. All I hadda do was shut up and wait. It happens every time.

"This queeb is Lippy's brother? I don't believe it!"

"Yeah, go and ask the Chief!"

Then Joe Crapanzano called them both over and they started talking. Well, Joe hadda act tough because his stooges were around, so he started squinting and spitting all over the place and he said, "I don't give two and a half shits whose brother he is!" He took out this tobacco pouch and a slip of yellow paper and he started rolling a cigarette just like a pro. And Jesus, he wasn't even ten years old! After he put away the pouch he said, "Hey, ginko, what's your name?"

"Me?" I said. Hymie musta thought I was crazy, acting wise like that, but I knew what I was doing. "Me?"

"Who d'ya think?" the third stooge said, watching Joe light up the cigarette and practically drooling. "What's ya name?"

"Benny. Benny Lipkowitz."

"I tol' ya the little bastard's Lippy's brother! . . . How old are ya?"

"Me? Seven an' a half."

"What's *his* name?" the second stooge said, pointing his finger at Hymie.

"Him? He's Hymie. Hymie Lipkowitz."

"Hey! How many brothers has Lippy got?"

"He's my cousin, not my brother."

"What's the diff? Give the kid back his immies, Lefty."

"You kidding!" the first stooge said. "It's the spoils of war! Ask the Chief!"

Joe Crapanzano just nodded once, the way Cagney or Raft

woulda done it, and the stooge gave the Band-Aid box back to Hymie. Then the stooge booted Hymie in the ass, but not too hard, and Joe gave me a short wink that was meant just for me. Nobody else noticed it. It takes a lotta practice to be able to wink like that. That's style! Then they all left.

"Lousy bastards," Hymie said, and now he started to cry, but not until he finished counting all his puries. And then he gets all excited and he wants to know how come I told the Assassins his name was Hymie Lipkowitz!

"What a dope you are, Hym, I swear. If they woulda found out you wasn't a Lipkowitz, your guts would be hanging out in the street. Lipkowitz, that's a magic name around here!"

Hymie's a little stubborn, and I guess that's because he's proud of his name. Sure, Moskowitz is a pretty nice name, I'm not saying no, but it's nothin next to Lipkowitz, and that's a fact! Ask anybody. From Freeman Street to Wilkins Avenue, from Crotona Park to Southern Boulevard, everybody that's anybody knows the Lip! There's just one name at P.S. 61 that counts more than Lipkowitz, and that's Crapanzano! The name Crapanzano is known all over the East Bronx, but that's because of Joe's brother Andy, the gangster, who once cut off a woman's tit and used it for a pillow. What do you want from Lippy, he can't compete with guys like that. Anyway, there's only two Lipkowitzes that go to P.S. 61, Lippy and me. And there's six Crapanzanos, and they're all killers, even the girls. There's Marie, Frankie, Junior, Tillie, Winkie, and Joe. Pound for pound, the Crapanzanos are the toughest family in the world. What a tribe! There's thirteen of 'em altogether, counting Rocco and Julio, who are up in the Pen. Sometimes I wish I was a

Crapanzano too, but I wouldn't want to be one if it meant being a goy.

Well, Hymie counted his puries again, and he said one was missing, so what the hell, I gave him one of mine. Anything to keep him from bawling. He wanted to know what "Ass-ass-in" means, and I told him it meant Killer or something, because I read it somewhere in Pinocchio. Then we walked home. We live on Seabury Place and the Crapanzanos live on Charlotte Street, one block away. My mother wasn't home so I went up to the roof and down the fire escape. Lippy broke the lock on the kitchen window for me and that's how I get in all the time. My mother says she'll kill me if she ever catches me doing it, but she always forgets to leave me the key. She works in the dress shop downstairs, and I feel like a dope going in there all the time and asking her for that lousy key. And the guy that owns the shop, Mister Fox, he hates me and I hate him. Well, he don't really hate me, he hates Lippy, but anybody that hates Lippy gotta hate me too! The Lipkowitzes are a tribe, just like the Crapanzanos, and we stick together. So I went in through the window and took some cornflakes with raisins and milk and I made a mustard sandwich. Everybody thinks I'm crazy for liking mustard so much, even Lippy, but I can't help it. And since when is eating mustard sandwiches a crime? I aint harming nobody by doing it. Then I read a comic. Wonder Woman was fighting off a whole team of African Amazons and that's when my mother came in. Right away she started in on me. And I'm her darling too. "What'd I do, raise up a monkey!" she said. "Climbs through windows. Remember, someday you'll fall off and— Where's Leo?"

Well, I figured I'd stall her a little, so I started going through my coughing and sneezing bit, but I knew it wouldn't work. My mother's no dope!

"What has he got there, a whole factory in his nose!"

She took a tissue and started squeezing my nose with it and she said, "Where's Leo? Talk!"

I got her to take the tissue away from my nose, and then I said, "I don't know, Ma. He didn't tell me nothin."

"You want me to call up Uncle Max?"

I thought maybe she was just throwing off a bluff, so I said, "Ma, have a heart, Leo'll be back in a minute, you'll see!"

"No," she said, "no!" And this time she wasn't bluffing or nothin. "How much can I stand? I'm asking you? Oy, is this a Leo! A regular gangster! Who knows what he's up to? And you're his spy! . . . No, I'm sending for Uncle Max." I saw it was too late already to stop her, but I figured I'd give it a try for Leo.

"Ma," I said, and I grabbed ahold of her pocketbook like we were playing a game of tug-a-war. But she pulled the pocketbook outa my hand. Nothin can stop my mother when she gets something into her head. And she said, "Benny, you're no better, Benny." And then she left.

There's only one person in the whole world that gives Lippy the creeps, and that's Uncle Max! I aint saying Lippy's afraid of him, but he likes it a whole lot better when Uncle Max aint around. Well, I wished there was a way I could signal Lippy, but what's the use, I knew he was gonna catch it. I hadda do something, so I took out my siddur and I kissed both covers twice and then I said

a coupla prayers Schwartzie taught us. I didn't know what
they meant, but I figured that if I said them hard enough
maybe they'd get to God. What's God for, anyway, if you
can't pray to Him or nothin? Then I said a coupla prayers of
my own and I put the siddur away. All of a sudden I didn't
feel so bad. Sure, Uncle Max's a killer, but Lippy's plenty
tough. He knows how to take care of himself.

When my mother got back, I figured I'd work on her a
little, so I washed all the dishes for her and dusted the walls
and I acted like a little angel. But it didn't help much. My
mother knows the score! "*Mamser*," she called me. "Uncle
Max will be here in a minute!" Ten minutes passed and
Uncle Max didn't show up, so I thought maybe my mother
was bluffing after all. If she was, it was a masterpiece! I
heard a noise in the hall and I knew right away it was Uncle
Max. Nobody walks like him! It sounds like the ape man.
So when he knocked on the door and my mother let him in,
I wasn't surprised or nothin. He didn't bother saying hello.
Uncle Max is always in a hurry. "Where is he, where?" he
said, and he started snooping around like a bulldog.
"Where?" He looked in all the closets and under every bed.
He even opened up the dumbwaiter door. "I catch him I'll
kill him. Henya, he'll ruin my business, Henya!" Uncle Max
owns a grocery store near Boston Road and the way he talks
about it somebody might think it was the most important
place in the world. More important than the White House.
"Henya, I hear they don't dare let him in the five-and-ten
any more. He steals everything! Where is he, Henya?
Once and for all, I'll kill him!"

Then I looked at my mother and I could see she knew

already she made a mistake calling Uncle Max. "Max," she said, "sit down, Max. He's not here yet. Max, it could be he only went with a friend? . . . Maybe you should go home?"

"Go home, she tells me, go home! It's all your fault, Henya, you let him go on the loose. It's time now for a little action!"

Well, I knew I should keep my mouth shut, but I couldn't help it, so I said, "Leo didn't do nothin wrong, Uncle Max. He went on an errand for Schwartzfarb, I swear it, I—"

"You shut up, you! You I can't stand altogether. At least Leo's a mensch! Leo don't tell lies!"

"Ma, tell him to lemme talk. I didn't wanna say nothin before, but Schwartzie's sick. He had one of his attacks. And Leo hadda go all the way downtown and get some medicine for him. You can ask Hymie Moskowitz if you—"

"You deaf?" Uncle Max said, and he started rolling up his sleeves. "Should I teach you what shut up means?"

"Max, let him talk. Benny, it's true? Schwartzfarb is sick?"

"I should die on the spot if I'm telling a lie. . . ."

"Don't worry," Uncle Max said, still rolling up his sleeves. "This I can arrange for you, easy! Lie or no lie!"

"Max, shah! Benny, tell me, Benny."

"I swear it, Ma. He's sick, he's sick! He even told me to tell you not to make any kishgah for him this week."

"Kishgah she makes for him. That schnorrer!"

"Max, maybe I should go and see how he is?"

"No!"

"Max, he's all alone, Max. He's got nobody. . . ."

"No, I said. Let him hire a nurse! You stay here until Leo comes!"

There's nobody in the world who can talk my mother

down, except Uncle Max. It's funny the way she always
listens to him. Maybe it's because she's a little afraid of him,
but I don't think so. Anyway, he's her big brother and everything, and he used to look after her a lot when they came to
America. That's what she's always telling me. "Where would
I be now without Uncle Max?" You know, crap like that! I
don't care what anybody says, something's fishy somewhere.
All I know is he took President Roosevelt's picture off the
wall in his store. And he's making so much money now that a
lotta people think he's turning into a Republican. I even
heard somebody say once that Uncle Max likes Governor
Dewey, but I don't think he's that much of a schmuck!
Everybody knows that President Roosevelt is the greatest
person in the world. Roosevelt! That's a magic name, like
Crapanzano or Lipkowitz.

Well, Uncle Max finished rolling up his sleeves and then
he sat down on one of the broken chairs in the kitchen. I
wished to God the chair'd cave in or something, but I knew
it wouldn't. God don't listen to wishes like that! But right
away I stopped worrying because I know God likes Leo and
He wouldn't let nothin bad happen to him. That's a fact!
Don't ask me how I know it, I just do. God don't care much
for sissies and fags. He likes guys that cut up a little. And if
Joe Crapanzano was a Jew, I'll bet He'd like him almost as
much as He likes Leo. Anyway, it was no use standing
around in the kitchen, I couldn't help Leo or nothin, so I
went into my room and put on the radio. It aint really my
room, it's Leo's, but he lets me sleep in it too. I knew I
wouldn't enjoy listening to the radio while I was worrying
about Leo, but the Fat Man was coming on in half a minute,
and I figured if I got interested in the story maybe I

wouldn't worry so much. But it didn't work. So I turned the radio off and I just sat on my bed. It was beginning to rain, and I got up off the bed and closed the window all the way down. Leo's got the leakiest room in the world. No matter what you do, rain's always coming in. I watched the super's cat run in the rain and hide behind a garbage can across the street, but I kept getting splashed, so I pulled down the shade and walked away from the window. I took out a comic from the box under my bed, but it was no use. I couldn't read or nothin. And it was a Classic Comic too! The rest of the comics stink, except Captain Marvel and Dare Devil. Leo likes the Classics, but he don't like the guy who draws them up. That's the way Leo is. He won't like a comic no matter how good it is, unless it's drawn the right way. Leo's making a comic of his own, but I don't know too much about it. All I know is it's gonna be called The Daggers and it's supposed to be about Joe Crapanzano's big brother Andy and his gang.

I heard a noise coming from the kitchen. I knew it was Leo. He musta tried to sneak up through the fire escape. I ran into the kitchen and there was Uncle Max pulling Leo by the hair. Leo was all wet, and my mother was screaming, and I felt like shit. Maybe if I woulda stayed in the kitchen all the time, I coulda warned Leo or something. Well, I figured the hell with it, whatever happens happens, so I tried to tackle Uncle Max, but he pushed me away with one hand and said, "Wait, you'll get it too!" And it's a funny thing, but Leo didn't fight back or nothin, he just let Uncle Max drag him around by the hair. He looked a little funny in his jacket, like he got fat all of a sudden. He had a bigger belly than Santa Claus, I swear! And all the time Uncle

Max was pulling his hair he kept trying to hold up his belly. Right away I knew the score. I just prayed that Uncle Max wouldn't make him open up his jacket. Uncle Max is a little blind in one eye, and he don't see too good from up close. And my mother was too excited to notice anything. She just kept screaming, "Max, Max, you'll pull out all his hair!" Finally Uncle Max let up and Leo just stood there holding up his belly. His head musta hurt like hell from all that hair pulling, but he didn't show it or nothin. Joe Crapanzano or no Joe Crapanzano, nobody's got style like Leo! And then Uncle Max started in with his Gestapo tactics. "So talk! Where were you!"

"No place," Leo said. And I knew he was gonna catch it good, so I said, "Lippy, tell him about Schwartzie," and then Uncle Max reached out and tried to pull some of my hair but I ducked and hid behind my mother. And it's a lucky thing for him he didn't get ahold of me, because Leo wouldn't let nobody touch me, not even Uncle Max. Leo's a killer when anybody starts up with me. All Uncle Max said to me was, "Wait, I'll fix your wagon too," and then he went back to Leo. "Talk, I'm telling you, talk! Where were you?" He started pulling Leo's hair again, but this time my mother stopped him. "Max, he's soaked through. He'll catch pneumonia on me. Let him change his clothes."

"First he'll do a little talking. I should let a little snotnose like that ruin my business? People must think he steals merchandise for me. He doesn't move until he talks!"

I saw it was gonna be like the battle of the giants, because Uncle Max wasn't gonna let up for no money, and there's no one in this world who's more stubborn than Leo when he wants to be, so there was nothin for me to do but stay near my mother and watch. Leo had it pretty rough because he hadda keep away from Uncle Max and hold up his belly at the same time. And if you think it's easy, try it sometime! It looked like Uncle Max was gonna win for sure, but Leo's terrific when the odds are against him. That's why it don't pay to start up with him. Because the worse you make it for him, in the end the worse it's gonna be for you! Well, I was waiting for Leo to make a move because it was getting pretty bad. Soon he wouldn't have any hair left. The only thing that saved him was my mother butting in.

"Max, you'll make him a baldy! Let him go in and change his clothes. . . . Max, Max! . . ."

But it was no use, because Uncle Max was all worked up, and he wouldn't let Leo move from the spot. "Talk, I said, talk!"

"I aint got nothin to say."

"Henya, give me the green light, I'll kill him!"

"Max, please."

"Don't beg him, Ma. He aint hurting me."

Maybe Leo shouldna said that, because this time Uncle Max gave such a pull on Leo's hair that I thought he was gonna tear his whole head off. "Don't make me ask you again. Tell me . . . where were you?"

Leo looked Uncle Max straight in the face and then he said, "Suck moose." Just like that.

Uncle Max punched Leo right in the nose. I don't think Joe Louis coulda hit harder than that! And Leo couldn't do nothin but hold up his belly. Lucky thing he was leaning against the window sill or it woulda been a knockout for sure. Leo's nose started bleeding and when Uncle Max saw the blood he calmed down a little. But then my mother started screaming. "It's murder! . . . He killed my Leo he killed . . ."

Uncle Max was beginning to get a little worried. "Shah, Henya, it's nothing . . . shah!"

"Leo, Leo!"

"Henya, *zei shtill!* The neighbors, they'll think God knows what happened! . . . Leo, tell her it's nothing, Leo, tell her . . ."

"I'm okay, Ma," Leo said. He wasn't backing down. He just don't like it when my mother cries. "He couldn't hurt me."

"I better go," Uncle Max said. "I have to be back at the store, Leo, wipe off the blood from your nose . . . and don't think I'm finished with you. . . . Goodbye!"

I gave Uncle Max one of Leo's voodoo signs while he was putting on his hat and then he left.

"Leo," my mother said, "let me find something to wipe off your nose."

"It's okay, Ma. It stopped bleeding."

"It's stopping he says! Oy, it's coming out like a fountain! Benny, make him he should hold back his head."

My mother took out an old curtain from the hall closet and she started wiping Leo's nose with it. When she was finished half the curtain was covered with blood. Then she told Leo to go into his room and put on different clothes. I wasn't gonna miss this for nothin so I followed Leo. But he wouldn't take off his jacket. "Whatja following me around for?"

"I wanna see what you got under your jacket."

"I aint got nothin. Now get outa here!"

"Come on, Lippy. You can show me."

"I said get outa here!"

Well, I knew it wasn't gonna be an easy job to get him to show me, so I started in on something else. "Hey, Lippy, did he hurt you?"

"Uncle Max? Na!"

"I thought he was gonna knock you out or something the way he punched you."

"Yeah, I can take anything he can throw. I was hit harder than that already."

"You mean it, Lippy, when? . . ."

"Ahhh! . . . You 'member that time when I came home from school with a shiner and I told Ma that a gang of boogies from Boston Road beat me up? . . . Well, it wasn't no boogies that did it. It was Nick, the janitor from school."

"Nick gave you the shiner? Why didn't you tell somebody? He can get arrested for doing that. He aint allowed to go around hitting kids."

"He had a reason for doing it, dope! He caught me in the basement stealing light bulbs. And he kicked the crap outa me. But that's okay. We're friends now. He gives me free butts and everything."

Then I said, "What kinda punch was it, Lippy, that gave you the shiner?"

Leo put up his hands and started to show me, but something fell outa the bottom of his jacket. I picked it up quick. "Holy shit," I said, "it's a silk stocking! Where the hell did you get it, Leo? It must be worth a fortune. Hey Lippy, let's go into the black market business. We can—"

"Shut up! Now gimme it and get the hell outa here."

"Who you gonna sell it to, Lippy?"

"I aint gonna sell it to nobody. I got it for Ma." Then he

put his hand inside his jacket and he pulled out a whole bundle of stockings. "They're all for Ma. I don't steal things to sell them back. I aint no lousy thief! Now you don't say nothin about this to nobody. You gotta help me think up a way to give 'em to her without her finding out where I got 'em."

"Where *did* you get 'em, Lippy?"

"Hey, mind your business, huh? Just start thinking."

"I don't know, Lippy. I aint no genius. Maybe we can mail 'em to her and say they came from Uncle Jack in Detroit."

"Na, she'd find out it's a lie. Hey, maybe I can tell her I got 'em in a fire sale. You think so, Benny?"

"Yeah, I never heard of anybody giving out silk stockings in a fire sale."

"All right. You hide 'em for me. We'll think of something later."

Well, I hid the stockings inside the giant jack-in-the-box that my Unce Jack sent me from Detroit a coupla years ago for Chanukah. Then Leo opened up his jacket and took out three big boxes of cigars. "Wow," I said, "wow, who's that for, Lippy?"

"For Gran'pa."

"All three boxes?"

"Well, I was gonna save one box for Uncle Max. But the hell with him now! We'll smoke 'em ourselves!"

Leo dumped the cigar boxes into the jack-in-the-box and I closed up the cover tight. "Oh, I forgot, Leo, you got anything else to put inside?"

"Yeah," Leo said, so I took off the cover again and then Leo put his hands inside his pockets and he pulled out two big bags filled up to the top with bubble gum.

"Holy holy shit!" That's all I could say. "Real bubble gum!
What'd you do, Lippy, rob some kind of a bank? . . . We
can make a fortune selling it, Lippy. It'll go for a nickel
apiece, at least. I can sell twenty-five pieces to Hymie
Moskowitz right now!"

"You aint selling nothin to nobody! If you wanna give him
a coupla pieces, okay. But no selling."

"Well, whatja gonna do with two whole bags? That's more
than a year's supply."

"We'll keep some of it and give the rest to Gran'pa."

"Gran'pa can't chew bubble gum. He aint got no teeth."

"Then I'll give it away. To Joe Crap and his brothers and
sisters. We'll see. Now put it away before Mommy comes
in."

There's no use arguing with Leo, he just aint got no sense
when it comes to making money, so I put the bubble-gum
bags on top of the cigars and I closed the cover again.

"I got something else," Leo said, "but I can keep it in my
pocket."

"What else you got, Leo?"

"Don't worry, it aint nothin for you. It's for Mommy. And
Gran'pa too. I got some ration stamps. Now Mommy can
buy all the sugar and meat she wants."

"You can get in real trouble for swiping them, Leo. That's
messing around with the Gov'ment. President Roosevelt can
send the F.B.I. after you for that. You better bring 'em back!"

"I aint bringing nothin back. Mommy needs 'em, so just
shut up with your F.B.I. I don't give a shit who they send
after me."

"All right, Lippy, I was only trying to look out for you,
that's all."

"I don't need you to look out for me, Benny. Look out better for yourself."

It's no use talking to Leo when he gets mad like that, so I just shut up and sat on my bed. Leo took off his pants and his shirt and he put them on the radiator. Then he stood around in his underpants and undershirt and did about seventy-five pushups. Leo's got terrific muscles. He does all the Charles Atlas exercises and he's saving up to buy some weights. We got a set of springs at home, but Leo don't like to use them because they're my father's. "Leo," I said, "you wanna work out, me and you?"

"No. Just sit there and shut up."

When his shirt and pants got a little dry, Leo put them back on. Then he said to me, "You stay here. I'm gonna talk to Mommy for a minute."

Leo came back in a little while. He still looked mad so I shut up.

"Whatja looking at me for?"

"Me, Lippy? I aint looking at nobody."

"You wanna know, I gave Mommy the stamps."

"She took 'em from you?"

"Sure she took 'em. She needs 'em, you dope! I told her I won 'em off some of the Assassins in a crap game. And I promised her I won't play crap no more, so everything's all right. Just shut up about it."

"Wow, what a story! She believed you was shooting crap for ration stamps?"

"Yeah, yeah, you know Ma. I told her none of us had no money so we used ration stamps. At first she told me to give the stamps back to the kids I won 'em from because otherwise their mothers'd be short. But then I told her that the

Assassins stole the stamps they had from other kids, so there was no use giving 'em back, and then she agreed to take 'em."

"You oughta be a lawyer, Lippy. You got real talent."

"Ah, when it's time to talk, I know what to say, that's all. There's nothin special about that."

Then Leo sat on his bed and started reading a comic, but he musta got tired reading pretty quick, because he put it down after the first page. "Hey Benny, you got a Classic Comic for me, huh?"

"Sure, which one? I got Ivanhoe, and Robin Hood, and The Count of Monte Cristo, and A Tale of Two—"

"Gimme Ivanhoe. I aint read that yet."

So I gave Leo Ivanhoe and he started reading again. But I wasn't doing nothin, so I said, "Lippy, how's your comic book coming?"

"What comic book?"

"You know, the one you're writing about Andy Crapanzano."

"How d'you know I'm doing a comic book about Andy Crap, huh? You been snooping around my stuff or what?"

"I aint been snooping nowhere, Leo. I saw you when you was working on the first page, don't you remember?"

"Okay, when I'm finished I'll show it to ya. Now lea' me alone."

I shut up for about a minute and then I said, "Hey Lippy, is it true that Andy Crapanzano uses a woman's tit for a pillow?"

"How should I know. Ask Joe. . . . Who told you that bullshit anyway?"

"I don't know, a lotta kids. And they all live on Charlotte Street too. So maybe it aint bullshit, Lippy, huh?"

"Hey Benny, how the hell can I read if you keep talking? Shut up!"

"Just one more thing, Lippy, and then I'll shut up for the whole night, I swear. . . . You know any stories about Andy, huh? Just tell me one little story and I won't bother you no more."

"I aint telling you no stories or nothin. And you open your mouth once more and I'm gonna stomp on your balls."

Leo don't bluff, so I shut up fast. But it's hard to keep quiet, especially when you know somebody wants you to, because you get a funny feeling in your mouth, like it's gonna explode unless you open it and say something. But I wasn't gonna take no chances with Lippy around, so I just put my head under my pillow and I whispered out a few words and then I felt better. Leo finished the comic in about ten minutes and then he said, "I'm going to sleep." And when Leo goes to sleep I gotta go to sleep too, because the light's gotta go out and I can't do nothin much in the dark. Leo took off his pants and his shirt and his shoes and he started putting on his pajamas, but I figured I'd stall him a little, so I said, "Don't you want me to do your homework for you, Leo?" That always works because Leo never does his own homework, and if I don't do it for him, it never gets done. My mother says that it's Leo who should be in the third grade, not me. But Leo's pretty smart, even if he don't do no school work. "Huh Leo, don't you want me to do it for you?"

"The heck with it," Leo said, and then he put out the

light, so I had to undress in the dark. I promised myself I wouldn't do Leo's homework for the next three weeks just for that, but I knew I wouldn't keep the promise. Well, I figured there was nothin left for me to do but go to sleep, so I closed my eyes. And I tried not to think about nothin, because you can't sleep that way. But I couldn't help it. I started thinking about my father. For a minute I made believe I was him and I tried to feel how it was like to be dead. At first it felt all right, because it didn't hurt or nothin, but then I got the creeps. It started in my toes and went up my legs and right through my belly and reached all the way up to my brain, and I knew it must be a terrible thing to be dead, and I couldn't help it, but I started to cry. Leo heard me.

"Whatja crying for?"

"Nothin, Lippy . . . I was thinking about *Deddy*."

Leo put on the light and he could see I was shivering a little. He cursed me a coupla times and he took his pillow and walked over to my bed. "You want me to sleep wicha?"

"Wouldja, Lippy, then I wouldn't be scared no more."

"Move over."

I moved all the way over to the left side of the bed, because Leo needs a whole lotta room. And I let Leo have most of the blanket. I didn't mind being cold, as long as Leo was there. Then Leo said, "Whatja gotta go and think about *Deddy* for? You can't help him or nothin. . . . You still crying or what?"

"No, I just wish I was old enough to go out an' kill every Nazi in the world."

"It wasn't the Nazis what killed him, it was the Japs."

"I know, Lippy, I know. But I still hate the Nazis more. If

they ever got a chance to come over here they'd kill Mama
and Gran'pa first thing."

"Yeah, well they better not count on it with me around!
And stop thinking about such things, huh? Go to sleep!"

"I can't, Lippy. . . . I just can't sleep. Couldja tell me a
story maybe?"

"You starting in? You want me to go back to my bed,
huh? . . . Awright."

"About Andy Crapanzano! Just one little story, Lippy,
then I'll go to sleep, I swear!"

"How many times I gotta tell ya? I don't know nothin
about Andy!"

"Well, then make something up, I don't care. Just say
whatever you wanna say."

"You know I don't like to tell a bullshit unless there's a
special reason for it, but I know a little about Andy Crapanzano from what Joe told me, and if you promise to go to
sleep right after I tell it, maybe I can make up a story for
you. . . ." Just then, when Leo was thinking about how to
start the story, my mother came in.

"Boys," she said, "boys, what's the occasion, two in one
bed!"

"It's nothin, Ma, Leo's gonna tell me a story."

"Stories in the middle of the night! Leo, go back to your
bed, Leo. Let Benny sleep. . . . You didn't cause enough
trouble for one day?"

Well, Leo didn't wanna cut up or nothin, so he hustled
back to his bed.

"*Shluff*, boys! Tomorrow you have to get up early to see
Zaide."

My mother made Leo put out the light and then she walked out of the room and closed the door. Leo got up and tiptoed in the dark back to my bed. I started to say something, but Leo held my mouth and he said in a whisper, "Shut up, you little fuck! You wanna bring her back? She'll call in the Bulldog after me again." We were quiet for a minute and we could hear my mother ironing in the kitchen. Then Leo said, "Listen, because I gotta speak low. . . . Andy Crapanzano is the meanest son-of-a-bitch alive, but one thing, he aint no bully. He don't pick on little kids or old men or nothin. So you don't have to be afraid of him if you see him. It's only big guys like me that he likes to start up with. And Andy always carries a knife around with him. He wouldn't go nowhere without it. He even keeps it on him when he sleeps. It's a push-button and it's got a blade like you never saw in your life. Anyway, when Andy was a little kid he had a friend named Frankie Rizeka who lived on Charlotte Street too. Andy and this kid Frankie always hung around together. Wherever Andy went, Frankie Rizeka went with him too. That's the way it was. They rode on freight cars, they stole lemons and oranges from the fruit stands on Jennings Street, and they fought off whole tribes of boogies from Boston Road. One day they went hunting for catfish in the Bronx River, and Andy fell in the water and almost drowned. One thing about Andy, he can't swim to save his ass! So Frankie Rizeka jumped right in and dragged Andy out. It was winter too and Frankie caught pneumonia. Andy felt like a double-barreled schmuck for falling in the water and making Frankie catch pneumonia. And he made Frankie a promise that if ever Frankie was in trouble he'd come and help him no matter what. Even if it meant killing somebody and getting the electric chair for it. Well, a little later, Frankie and his father moved up to Fordham Road, and now him and Andy couldn't see each other so much, so they hadda stop being such good friends. Anyway, Frankie joined up with the Fordham Baldies, and pretty soon he stopped seeing Andy altogether. You know, that's the way everything is. . . ."

It was a terrific story and I wished it'd never finish, so I said, "Whatja stopping for, huh Lippy?"

"I'm thinking," Leo said, "I'm thinking. . . . Well, Frankie Rizeka was plenty tough, and when he got a little bigger, they made him the chief of all the Baldies. And you know what bastards the Baldies are, they start up with everybody. And one day a buncha Baldies came all the way over to Crotona Park and they took Joe Crap and threw him in the lake. Joe was only five when it happened, so he couldn't fight back. When Andy heard about it he was mad as hell. He took Joe back with him to the park and he made him point out the Baldies who threw him into the lake. Then Andy kicked their asses in three at a time, and he carved a little x on their foreheads with his knife. And he told the Baldies to stay the hell outa his territory from now on. Andy figured there was gonna be trouble, and he knew he couldn't handle all the Baldies by himself, they're the biggest gang in the Bronx, so he came back the next day with his big brothers Rocco and Julio, that was before they were sent off to Sing Sing, and with all his cousins from Charlotte Street. He also rounded up Stanley Schapiro and his boys from Longfellow Avenue to help out. Well, about five hundred Baldies showed up, and it looked like it was gonna be a massacre because every hill around the lake was.

covered with Baldies, and all of them had garrison belts or
lead pipes or sticks with nails at the end. But you don't gotta
worry about the Crapanzano boys, because one Crapanzano
is worth a hundred Baldies, easy! And don't forget, Stanley
Schapiro was also there, that was the clincher! Well, the
fight started and the Baldies charged down from the hills
shouting the Baldy war song, but the Crapanzanos didn't
move an inch."

"Wow," I said, "wow!"

"Shut up, huh Benny! How can I tell a story if you start
interrupting me? So shut up! . . . Well, Baldies kept getting knocked into the lake right and left, but one Baldy there
fought like a maniac. He had a lead pipe and he almost took
Stanley Schapiro's head off with it. It was Frankie Rizeka.
Andy recognized him right away. And pretty soon all the
Baldies retreated back to the hills and they left Frankie
Rizeka standing there alone swinging his pipe. Rocco and
Julio were gonna charge him, but Andy said no. He remembered his promise. 'Go home, Frankie,' Andy said, 'go
home.' But Frankie wouldn't listen or nothin. Maybe the
other four hundred and ninety-nine Baldies are a buncha
faggots, but not Frankie Rizeka. Well, Andy didn't wanna
send Rocco or Julio after Frankie, because they woulda
slaughtered him, and he couldn't ask Stanley to fight him,
because maybe Stanley woulda got hurt, so there was nothin
else he could do. He hadda fight Frankie himself. Andy's a
killer with his knife, but he didn't want Frankie to get cut
up, so he put it away and he started fighting with his hands.
But Frankie still had his pipe, and he kept knocking Andy
over the head with it, so Rocco and Julio started shouting,

'Andy, use the shiv!' But Andy made up his mind already he wasn't gonna use his knife, so he kept getting bopped over the head, and all the Baldies on top of the hills kept cheering for Frankie. Finally Rocco and Julio said 'Fuck it' and they stopped the fight and took turns kicking the shit outa Frankie. They even hit him over the head with his own lead pipe. Frankie wasn't no match for Rocco and Julio, nobody is! Then they took Andy home. Joe tells me that Andy kept crying the whole night because he couldn't keep his promise to Frankie, but he was still glad that he didn't use his knife on him."

"What happened to Frankie, huh Lippy?"

"I don't know. Nobody ever saw him after that. Now go to sleep!"

Well, my mother woke me and Leo up early in the morning, and she already had the latkahs and kishgah and kreplach wrapped in a big brown bag for Gran'pa, and the way it looked, she musta worked all night. Me and Leo brushed our teeth and got dressed and ate breakfast. Leo finished eating a little before me, and while my mother was still in the kitchen, he opened the jack-in-the-box and snuck two boxes of cigars into the big brown bag. It musta been heavy as hell to carry, but Leo didn't mind it one bit. My mother gave me and Leo thirty-five cents apiece, because we had to take a bus and a train to get to Gran'pa, and we still had a little money left over to spend on candy or halvah. My mother let Leo hold all the money, because she thinks I can't hold onto money without losing it or something, and that gets me mad, but I didn't wanna say nothin, or otherwise we woulda never got started. "Leo, take care," my mother said. "Hold his hand when you cross the street, Leo, promise me. He's still a baby yet."

Leo hadda promise and then we left. He wanted to walk across to the West Bronx instead of taking the bus. That way we could save a nickel both ways. I hate to walk across Crotona Park because all the colored kids hang out there, but I don't mind it so much when I'm with Leo. So we started walking. When we got to Boston Road and started to cross over, Leo held onto my hand. "Cut it out, Lippy, huh?" I said, and I was really getting mad. "You want people to think I'm a sissy or something?"

"I promised Mommy, so I gotta do it," Lippy said, and he gripped my hand so tight I thought all my fingers were gonna fall off. When we got to Crotona Park Leo told me to be on the lookout for any gangs of colored kids. Leo wasn't scared or nothin, but he didn't want no funny business because of the latkahs and everything he was carrying. "Boogies love latkahs," that's what Leo said. So while we were walking I looked both ways but I didn't see no boogies. It was too early in the morning. Well, we crossed over Crotona Park without nobody bothering us. But wait, we still hadda get past Third Avenue and Washington Avenue and Claremont Park, and that's where a lotta colored kids hang out. Leo has all the luck, because we got to the Grand Concourse, and everything was still okay. We went down into the subway and we took the "D" train and Leo let me sit near the window. We hadda ride a long way, so I asked Leo to tell me more about Andy Crapanzano, but Leo told me to shut up. I sat on my seat and I kept quiet all the way down to Delancey Street.

Then we got off the train and left the underground. We could see the Williamsburg Bridge and everything. Once Gran'pa took me and Leo halfway across the bridge. We wanted to go all the way over, but it started to rain, so we hadda go back. Maybe Gran'pa was gonna take us somewhere today. To Chinatown or the Bowery where all the bums hang out and where Uncle Max says Leo's gonna end up. Leo bought a knish for a nickel outa his money and he gave me half. One thing about Leo, he aint cheap! Then he lemme buy a big piece of halvah for three cents outa my money and I shared it with him. When we got to Clinton Street, where the bridge starts, we turned to the left. Leo still held onto my hand when we crossed the street, but I didn't mind it so much now, because I didn't know anybody down here. We passed a coupla rebbes with big beards and black suits and also a lotta kids with yamulkas on and with payis hanging down from their ears. I don't like to say it, but they look funny as hell. And lucky thing for these kids that they live down here, because if they walked around my neighborhood like that they wouldn't last a minute! Gran'pa says it's the ghetto down here and everything goes! Yamulkas, payis, and beards! Gran'pa's supposed to be a big man down here. My mother says he used to write poems and articles for all the Jewish newspapers, but I don't believe it. How come if he's such a big man he has to live in a dump on Henry Street? Anyway, me and Leo passed East Broadway and we could see the big sign on top of the building that puts out the *Forward*. That's the biggest Jewish newspaper in the world, and more people read it than the *News* or the *Mirror*, and that's a fact! And if Gran'pa used to write for it, then he must be a big man, but I don't know! Me and

Leo got to Henry Street and there was a coupla big kids
with yamulkas standing on the stoop outside Gran'pa's house
and they heckled us a little, but Leo didn't wanna start up or
nothin, on account of the latkahs. So we just walked right
past them and we went up to Gran'pa's. He lives on the
fourth floor, and every time you go through the halls it stinks
from cat's piss. What a place! When we got up to the fourth
floor Leo knocked on the door. Rivkeh opened the door for
us and she didn't smile or nothin. But that's okay, because
she's never too happy to see us. She's Gran'pa's second wife,
and we don't have to call her "bubbe" or nothin, just Rivkeh.
But when Gran'pa heard that it was us, he started jumping
up and down like some kind of a Chinese idiot. He grabbed
Leo around and he started dancing with him. And he kissed
me too. I have to admit it, Gran'pa's crazy about Leo. I
mean, he likes me too, but not like Leo. He'd die for Leo, I
mean it! And every time my mother takes me to see him
without Leo, Gran'pa asks, "Where's Leo?" and then he gets
a little mad and he don't talk to nobody, no matter how
many latkahs and kreplach my mother brings him. Well,
after Gran'pa finished dancing with Leo, he took us into
his room and he locked the door. He didn't want Rivkeh
to bother him or nothin. Leo took out the latkahs and we
had a feast. Then Leo took out the two boxes of cigars.
"That's for you, Zaide," Leo said. "Me and Benny saved up
for it, and we got it for cheap at a fire sale. Didn't we,
Benny?"

"Sure, sure," I said, but Gran'pa aint no dope. First he
pretended to be mad and everything, but I could see he
wanted to cry, because he knew Leo stole the cigars special
for him. "Leo," he said, "how can I take it? . . . You'll make

me your accomplice! How would it look for a zaide to end up in Sing Sing? . . . Leo, you promised me, no more stealing." But Gran'pa wasn't too hard on Leo. He aint a phony like Uncle Max. He knows that Leo aint no crook. If he steals, maybe there's a special reason for it. Leo never stole a thing when my father was alive. I don't remember, but that's what Gran'pa says. And he don't tell bullshit stories. "Leo . . ."

"Ah, take 'em, Zaide," Leo said. "I can't bring 'em back anyway. And what's the use of letting good cigars rot!"

Gran'pa shut up about the cigars and took out his Victrola. Leo never likes to sing except when we're with Gran'pa, so we all started dancing and singing Jewish songs. Then Rivkeh knocked on the door. "Stop the *tumel!* Mayshke, they'll bring up the landlord."

"Nudnick, go away!" Gran'pa said, and he opened the door and gave Rivkeh all the kreplach. "I never saw such a woman. All my enjoyment she wants to take away from me . . . go!" Gran'pa locked the door and we finished the song. He took out a big bottle of cherry wine and we all drank two glasses. Then Gran'pa warmed up the Victrola again, and this time he made up his own song.

Un az der Rebbe kakt, un az der Rebbe kvetcht,
Un az der Rebbe trent, tziteren di vent.

Gran'pa made believe he was the rebbe in his song, and he started dancing all over the place. And he dances like a devil for a guy his age. He took a little more wine and he started dancing again. Me and Leo were clapping for him and everything. But Gran'pa got a little dizzy and he hadda stop, and then Leo did the dancing for him. And Leo was

terrific! But he was making a lotta noise, and we thought
Rivkeh was gonna come back any minute. So Leo jumped up
on Gran'pa's bed and he finished off the dance there. Then
Gran'pa put on his coat and we all went downstairs. Gran'pa
went into the shul across the street and he started handing
out cigars to everybody. Then we went to the playground on
Straus Square. Gran'pa gave out a cigar to the parkman and
he went over to the chess table and started kibitzing with
some of the old guys there, but he didn't give out any cigars.
Me and Leo worked out on the chinning bar and the parkman let us play with the shuffleboard set. Meanwhile, Gran'pa
played a game of chess, then he came over to us and asked if
we wanted to go to the movies. But my mother said we
shouldn't let Gran'pa spend any money on us because he aint
got too much money himself, so Leo said no. But Gran'pa
could see that we wanted to go, and he said, "Wait." Then
he switched over from the chess table to the card table, and
when he won enough money to take us all to the movies, he
quit. The other old men didn't like the idea of him walking
off with their money, but I guess there was nothin they
could do about it. Anyway, Gran'pa took us to see two
Charlie Chan movies at the Delancey. Then we all went
back to Gran'pa's house. When we got upstairs Leo gave
Gran'pa the ration stamps. "Take 'em, Zaide," Leo said, "and
don't holler at me or nothin. You can use 'em!" So Gran'pa
took the stamps and didn't say nothin, and then he kissed
Leo and me and he said, "Leo, when are you coming to see
your zaide again?"

"Maybe next week," Leo said, and we said goodbye to
Rivkeh and then we left. We walked back to Delancey Street
and we went down into the subway and got on the train.

This time we went to the first car and I looked at all the colored lights in the tunnel. I put my hands over my ears and I heard a "wah-wah" sound like the seashore. But Leo made me cut it out, because he said I looked stupid. I had nothin to do so I started counting, and I counted up to five thousand and thirty-six when the train got to our station. Leo wanted to take the bus back, but I said no. "We walked here, and we can walk back!"

The sun was going down already, and when we got to Crotona Park it was almost dark. I saw a coupla colored kids coming and I wanted to run, but Leo said no. It never pays to run! I could see that these colored kids were looking for trouble, and I started to shake even with Leo there. But Leo wasn't scared or nothin, and they could see it too. They stopped me right away and they searched me. Leo told 'em to leave me alone, and then the biggest colored kid there walked over to him and pulled out an ice pick. I almost shit two bricks! "Hey, muh' fucker, what you mean, 'leave him alone!' "

Leo looked right in the colored kid's face and he said, "What's Big Daddy gonna say when he finds out you been messing around with us?"

That shook up the colored kid a little, I could see it. And he said, "Hey, muh' fucker, how you know Big Daddy, huh?"

"I don't know him," Leo said, " . . . but my brother does."

"Who dat?"

"Andy Crapanzano."

"Whitey," the big colored kid said to one of the other colored kids, "you evah heah of this Andy guy?"

"Yeah, ah heard of him. Big Daddy knows him. You beh'

leave these two muh' fuckers alone. Ah don' wan' no trouble with Big Daddy."

Then the big colored kid put his ice pick away. "Okay, get goin', and don' you say nothin 'bout this to Big Daddy, heah?"

Well, I wanted to get the hell outa there fast, but Leo said, "Slow, slow," so I walked behind him. When we got to the end of the park I said to Leo, "Who's Big Daddy, Lippy?"

"Ah, he's the head nigger around here. The big Chief. Nobody messes with him, except maybe Andy Crap."

Then I said to myself, "Big Daddy," and I started laughing. "No, we don' wan' no trouble with Big Daddy."

"You better shut up, Benny. You can't blame those boogies. Big Daddy's a killer. He don't need ice picks. That's for punks. He's got machine guns and everything. Even Andy Crap would think twice before messing around with him. Now shut up!"

When we got to Seabury Place we looked through the window of Fox's lousy sweatshop to see if my mother was still inside. She's always the first one in there and the last one out. Leo was gonna write "Eat Mung" all over Fox's window, but what's the use. Fox would know in a minute who did it, and then he'd make trouble for my mother. When my mother finds another job, he's gonna get the works! Anyway, my mother was near the back sweeping up the place, so Leo knocked on the window once to show her we were there. And Fox musta thought we were up to no good, because right away he came outside holding a broomstick. "Go away, go, before you catch *klep!*"

"I'm waiting for my mother," Leo said, and he didn't move an inch.

But my mother came outside and she made Leo move away. "No trouble, Leo. . . . Go upstairs. Benny, go with him, Benny, please . . ."

I could see my mother was working hard and everything, and it was stupid to start trouble, so I said to Leo, "Come on, Lippy, let's go." We went upstairs, and on the way up Leo said, "I'm gonna kill that lousy bastard one of these days," and I could see from the way he said it that he meant it. I made Leo a cream cheese sandwich and I made a mustard sandwich for myself. A little later my mother came up and she started in on Leo. "Leo, Leo, who can put up with you? Honest to God, the boy's impossible. . . . How's Zaide?"

"He's all right, Ma," I said. "And he loved the latkahs."

She looked at us. "Boys, did you take money from your Zaide?"

"Nah," I said, "nah." Leo was gonna say something, but he changed his mind.

Then I asked her, "How's Schwartzie, Ma?"

"Shah! Have a little respect. He's plenty sick, Benny. And it's no wonder when he has to handle boys like your brother. Benny, I made some chicken soup for him this morning. Maybe you'll bring it up to him later?"

"Sure, Ma, I'll go right now if you want."

"No, first eat!"

"I aint hungry, Ma. Gimme the soup. I'll eat when I get back."

My mother put the soup in a jar and then I took it with me. Schwartzie lives in the next house so I went up to the roof, because that's the easiest way to go. The roofs on my block are all attached. But when I opened the door that goes up to the roof I heard someone yell, "Chickee!" so I said, "Hey, it's only me, Benny Lipkowitz!" Then I saw Hymie

Moskowitz and Albie Saperstein coming out from behind a clothesline. Albie had his bee-bee gun.

"What're you guys doin up here, huh?"

"Shooting tin cans," Albie said.

"How come you were hiding behind the clothesline?"

"We thought you was the super or something. Whatja got in that jar, Benny?"

"Jar? Oh. It's soup for Schwartzie."

"Look, Hymie," Albie said, "Benny's Schwartzie's errand boy."

"You better shut up, Albie."

"You gonna make me?" Albie said. And he musta thought he was a big man because he had his bee-bee gun. "You come near me and I'm gonna shootja."

Albie's the biggest fag in the world, and he wouldn't shoot nobody unless it was a kid five years old, so I walked right up to him. "Whatja waitin for, shoot!" I don't wanna brag, but I got a little style too! "What's a matter, Albie, I aint a big enough target for you, huh?"

Albie put down the bee-bee gun and he said, "Yeah, I could kill you if I shotja. It's a Daisy Red Rider. And I don't wanna get arrested."

"Albie's right," Hymie said. "Red Riders can kill people."

"You shut up!" I said to Hymie, and I was mad enough to fight the two of them, but I didn't wanna spill the soup. So I just said, "Why is it that fags always stick up for each other?"

"Yeah," Albie said. "You think you're so big just because you're Lippy's brother. You know nobody's gonna start up wicha because they don't want no trouble with Lippy."

"I don't need Lippy to do my fighting. You want me to prove it to you?"

But Hymie's the head of the faggots' union, so he stepped between me and Albie and he said, "Albie aint looking for no trouble, Benny. Let's go find a cat to shoot!"

"No thanks. I don't go 'round pickin on cats. See ya." But then I remembered about all the bubble gum stashed at the bottom of the jack-in-the-box, so I said, "Anybody 'round here wanna buy some bubble gum?"

"Bubble gum," Hymie said, "you kiddin? You know you can't get no bubble gum because of the war. Even Albie's uncle Bernie can't get none, and he's a cop!"

"Yeah, all I know is I got a whole lot of bubble gum to sell."

"Where'd you get it, Benny, huh?"

"That's my business. Whatja tryin' to do, go 'round snooping for Big Bernie the cop? You wanna buy any?"

"How much you sellin it for?" Albie asked me.

"Ten cents apiece!"

"It aint worth it for ten cents apiece." That's what Albie said. But Hymie kept quiet.

"Don't do me no favors, Albie. If you don't wanna buy it, then don't. I'll bring a coupla pieces with me to Hebrew tomorrow, and that's all I'm gonna say." I took the jar and I walked over to the next roof. Schwartzie lives near the top floor, so I only hadda walk down one flight. I didn't wanna knock on his door too hard, because maybe he was sleeping or something. But the door was open, so I just walked in.

"Rebbe, it's me, Benny Lipkowitz." I didn't hear no answer, so I went right in his bedroom. Schwartzie was snoring away. He was wearing a nightgown like my mother wears sometimes and it looked funny as hell. But I didn't wanna wake him, so I didn't laugh or nothin. I put the soup on the little table near his bed, and there was some dirty dishes on it, so I took them into the kitchen and I washed them. Maybe if Lippy saw me he'd think I was a fag, but nobody was around, so it was okay. Then I looked in once more to see how Schwartzie was doing, and his blanket was coming off, so I put it on him again. I went out and I closed the door without making too much noise and I went back up on the roof. Well, I couldn't find Hymie and Albie or nothin, so I made believe I was Billy Conn getting ready to fight Joe Louis, and after I knocked out Joe Louis fifteen times, I went back down to my place. My mother wanted to know why it took me so long, and I didn't wanna tell her nothin about being on the roof, because nobody's supposed to go up there, so I told her I hadda warm up Schwartzie's soup for him and that's why it took so long. She wanted to know if Schwartzie liked the soup, and I said, "Yeah, the way he was drinking it, he coulda finished off a whole gallon, easy!" My mother always likes it when people praise her soup, so I didn't feel too bad telling such a lie. Then she made me a tuna fish sandwich and it tasted terrible, but I didn't wanna say nothin. Tuna fish comes out of a can, and it aint my mother's fault if it don't taste too good. When I finished eating I went into Leo's room. Leo was sitting on his bed all hunched over, and I could see he was doing something important. I took a peek over his shoulder. Wow, he was working on his comic book! I didn't want Lippy to think I was a sneak, so I said, "How's it goin, Lippy?" Right away Lippy covered up his work and he said to me, "Scram, Benny."

I hadda figure out something to do, so I decided right on the spot that I'd do a comic book of my own. I took out my colored pencils and I sharpened every one. "Hell," I said to

myself, "I'm gonna do a comic about Big Daddy!" But I
never drawed any colored people before, and it was a little
hard to do. I was gonna chuck the whole idea, but then I
decided to draw Big Daddy like a white guy and color him
in brown after I was all finished. I figured I'd do about a
hundred-page comic and sell it to Dell Comics because they
put out Donald Duck, or maybe if it was good enough I'd
even try to sell it to Classic Comics. But after I finished the
first page, I knew I was never gonna do a hundred pages. It
was hard as hell! It was after nine already when I finished
my second page, and if this was how long it was gonna take
me to do two pages, I wouldn't be finished before next year.
But one thing, I had fun doing it. I made Big Daddy the
king of the crooks in the Bronx, and I let me and Leo be his
henchmen. I was gonna put Andy Crapanzano in the comic
too, but I changed my mind. I didn't wanna copy from Leo,
so I left Andy out. And I put in Joe Crapanzano instead. I let
Joe be one of Big Daddy's henchmen too, but I put him
under me and Leo. He hadda take orders from us. When I
was about halfway through my third page, Leo stopped
working, so I figured I'd stop too.

"You wanna see my comic, Lippy? . . . I started one
while you was working. You wanna see it, huh?"

"No. Show it to me when you're all finished."

"Ah, come on, Lippy. Look at it! I don't know when it's
gonna be finished. It's about Big Daddy, Lippy. And I put
me and you in it too. But don't worry, I left Andy Crapanzano out. Come on, Lippy, who'm I gonna have to show it to
if you don't look at it?"

"All right, all right," Lippy said and he looked at it. He
laughed and everything while he was reading it. And it's a

good sign that Leo likes something when he laughs. "It's pretty good so far, Benny, but I don't like the way you made some of the drawings."

"Well, they aint supposed to be like real people, they're supposed to be funny."

"I know," Leo said. "You aint telling me nothin. I still don't like some of your drawings and it aint got nothin to do with being funny. You don't know how to shade in right. Your lines are too straight. But otherwise it's okay."

"Leo, will you help me out with it, huh? Will you show me how to do the shading and everything?"

"Yeah, but not now. I aint in the mood for it no more. I wanna listen to the radio."

The Saturday-night fights were on. Two middleweights were fighting, Tiny Axelrod and Tony Jomboline, and if you ask me, they both stink. But that's okay, because most of the good fighters are in the army. Like Joe Louis and Billy Conn. After the fight was over, I said to Leo, "Leo, you think Billy Conn's gonna take Joe Louis when they get outa the army, huh?"

"I don't think so, Benny, but he's got a good chance. Billy Conn can box like a son-of-a-bitch, but he aint got a punch like Joe Louis. I wish he'd win though. It'd be nice to have another Jewish champ."

"You sure he's Jewish, Leo? All the Irish fighters like to take Jewish names when they fight in New York."

Leo looked at me. "Billy Conn aint no lousy mick. He comes from Stebbens Avenue. Everybody knows that."

"I betja all the boogies are gonna bet on Joe Louis to win."

"Well, you can't blame 'em."

"You aint gonna bet on him, are you, Lippy?"

"Na, I aint betting on no boogy! I still say Billy Conn aint gonna win. But if he puts up a good fight, that'll be okay too."

"Hey Lippy, Big Bernie the cop told Albie that if Billy Conn stayed away from Joe Louis for the last two rounds, he woulda won the other fight."

"So what! That aint no way to win. If he couldn't win the right way, he didn't wanna win at all."

"Yeah, and Big Bernie says Ted Williams is better than Hank Greenberg, and everybody knows Hank Greenberg is the best player in baseball. Even Schwartzie says so! Nobody can hit homers like Hank Greenberg. Watta you think, Lippy, huh? Who's better?"

"I aint no expert. . . . You ask me, Joe DiMaggio's better than botha them."

"Joe DiMaggio? You kiddin, Lippy? I thought you hate the Yanks."

"I do, I do, but that don't mean nothin."

"Yeah, but he aint Jewish like Hank Greenberg. . . ."

"I wouldn't give a shit if he was a boogy even, nobody's got style like Joe DiMaggio."

Well, when Lippy said that, I figured it was time to give up. How can you talk to anybody who could like somebody even if he was a boogy? I mean, I aint got nothin against boogies, but a boogy's a boogy! And I don't care what Lippy says, Hank Greenberg's terrific! When he gets outa the army, Joe DiMaggio and everybody else better watch out. That's all I gotta say. Anyway, I went to sleep right after that, I didn't wanna talk to Leo or nothin. And when I woke up in the morning I was still mad as hell, and Leo could see it too.

"Whatja lookin at me like that for, Benny? You wanna kick in the teeth?"

Well, I figured what the hell, there aint no use being mad

at Lippy, he's my brother and everything, and he can think the way he wants, so I said, "I got a piece of dirt in my eye, Lippy, and the only way you can get it out is to stare at somebody and then blink three times."

But Lippy knew I was fulla crap and he told me to shut up. So while we were eating breakfast, I didn't open my mouth once except to put food in it. Maybe you'll think Leo's a baby when I tell you this, but sometimes my mother gotta feed him and everything or else Leo won't eat. Leo just don't like to eat, that's all, and he'd starve himself unless my mother forced him. "Eat, Leo, eat," she always says, and then she sticks the spoon right in Leo's mouth. Me, I eat like a general, that's what my mother says. But it aint nothin to brag about. There's nothin special about knowing how to eat. Well, I finished breakfast fast, and my mother kept after Leo. "Leo, you'll be late for Hebrew."

I figured I'd stick up for Leo, so I said, "How can there be Hebrew, Ma, if Schwartzie's sick?"

But my mother got on my tail right away. "Is this a bandit! Did you ever know a day when Schwartzfarb missed a class? . . . Finish up, Leo. *Shnell!*"

There was nothin else we could do, so while Leo finished eating, I sneaked over to the jack-in-the-box and loaded my pockets with bubble gum, and then we went to Hebrew. Sunday's an easy day because we don't hafta bring books or nothin, we just sit around all day and listen to Jewish programs on Schwartzie's radio. And then maybe we sing a coupla songs. But Leo always sneaks out before it comes time to sing. You should hear this radio program we always listen to. It's called *Tzuris bei Leiten*, and it's run by this guy Nuchum Shtutzcock. You think you got troubles, huh? Well, listen! Terrible things are always happening to people on this program. Zaides get heart attacks right and left and children keep sending their bubbes to old-age homes. And it's Schwartzie's favorite show! I don't think he would ever let a Sunday go by without listening to it. And he's always crying after the show is over. If you ever say a bad word about Nuchum Shtutzcock you're as good as dead! Anyway, we got to Hebrew, and Hymie Moskowitz and Albie Saperstein were waiting for me outside, so I told Leo I'd be up in a minute, and then me and Hymie and Albie started talking business. I figured I'd catch Hymie for a dollar, at least!

"You got the gum?" Hymie said, and he took out two dimes. "Gimme two."

"Two! I aint selling no two pieces. If you get up enough jack to buy ten, lemme know."

"Wait," Albie said, "gimme twenty-five."

"What?" I said, "what?"

"You heard me." I gotta admit, Albie's got a little style too, even if he is a schmuck with earlaps. "Come on, gimme twenty-five pieces."

I figured I'd stall him a little, so I said, "You got the jack to pay for it?"

"Sure," Albie said, and he counted out twenty-five dimes. He musta robbed somebody's piggy bank. But it didn't make no difference to me where his money came from. It's a lucky thing for me I brought along some extra pieces of bubble gum, otherwise I woulda lost some good trade. I gave Albie the twenty-five pieces, and then Hymie started nagging him.

"Come on, Albie, sell me one piece, huh?"

"Sure," Albie said, "sure . . . for twenty cents!"

Well, there was nothin Hymie could do, I wasn't gonna sell him any, and he was stuck right in the middle, so he hadda buy a piece from Albie for twenty cents. Then we all went upstairs. Something terrible musta happened to Schwartzie, because he wasn't there. And Seymour Pinkowitz and Lippy were cutting up like two Mongolian idiots. They were throwing chairs around and everything. And Seymour almost broke Schwartzie's radio too! Then he got up on top of Schwartzie's desk and he said, "Listen . . . listen . . . *Tzuris bei Leiten*," and everybody started cracking up, even Lippy. And it's hard as hell to make Lippy laugh. A funny little fat guy with a yamulka and a beard came up the steps, and Seymour thought it must be some big shot, so he got off the desk. Then the little fat guy waddled in like a duck, and without taking off his coat he told us that he was a rabbi from downtown and he was taking Schwartzie's place for the day. When we heard that, we figured we'd have some fun. We were waiting for Leo to give the signal. But Leo didn't say nothin, so I figured I'd break the ice for him. And I said, "Rebbe, we gonna hafta listen to *Tzuris bei Leiten?*"

"No," the rebbe said. "Today is lecture day."

"Lecture day?" Seymour Pinkowitz said. *"Phooey!"* And right away he made a coupla lip farts. But Lippy gave him a dirty look, so he stopped. The rebbe stood in front of Schwartzie's desk and he looked at all of us and then he clapped his hands and said, "Boys, the afflictions that are awaiting all of you, don't ask! . . . don't ask!"

No one knew what the hell the rebbe was talking about, so Seymour said, "What kind of a nut did they send us from downtown?"

Then the rebbe said, "Boys, is it possible that you never heard of Gehinnom?"

"Ge*what*om?" Seymour said.

"Gehinnom!"

None of us knew what Gehinnom was, but I raised my hand anyway and I said, "I know, Rebbe, I know. . . . Gehinnom, that's the place where they send troublemakers like us! There aint no candy or bubble gum or nothin in Gehinnom, you just walk around with a monkey's tail and a toad's face and they never let you out unless you promise to be good forever!" I figured maybe Gehinnom was something like the place where they sent Pinocchio and his boys. Anyway, we all started laughing like hell. Even Lippy laughed a little. But the rebbe, he didn't say nothin, he started twisting the hairs at the bottom of his beard and he let us laugh. Pretty soon we stopped laughing, because it wasn't funny no more. Then the rebbe stopped playing with his beard, and he smiled and told everybody that Gehinnom was a lot like the way I said it was.

Seymour started stamping his feet. "Hooray for Benny! Give him a medal! Hooray—"

But Lippy cut him off quick. "Shut up, Seymour! Let the rebbe talk!"

"Gehinnom *is* a place for punishment, but you don't go there when you are a little boy, or even when you are grown up . . . you go there only after you are dead."

Well, the rebbe started telling us about Gehinnom and it was pretty interesting, so we all listened. Even Seymour shut up. "Gehinnom," the rebbe said, "is somewhere in the west, and it's so hot there, it could burn holes in the sun." The rebbe made a hole with his hands and then he said, "Let me be plagued by demons if I am telling a lie!" Rebbes don't make statements like that unless they mean it, so we knew it was the truth. "Boys, do you know why the sun gets all red in the evening?"

Nobody knew the answer, and I couldn't think up something funny, so I said, "Why, Rebbe, why?"

"Because it passes over the entrance to Gehinnom."

"No shit!" Seymour said. "No shit!"

"Gehinnom has seven rooms and each room is filled with fire and wind and all kinds of terrible tortures. It makes me tremble whenever I think of it." And the rebbe trembled for us. "Even though Gehinnom is all on fire, it is darker there than the darkest night. No flashlight would ever work in Gehinnom. Boys, you can't see a thing."

"Who's in charge there, huh Rebbe?" Seymour said.

"Dumah," the rebbe said. "Dumah's in charge. He is a special angel and he travels around the world and he makes out big lists of all those people who are going to be thrown into Gehinnom after they die."

And then I asked the rebbe, "Rebbe, is Gehinnom for Jewish people only?"

He kept quiet for a minute. I know he was thinking real hard because he started pulling on his beard like a maniac, and then he said, "No!" Just like that.

"And once you are in Gehinnom, you can never get out. It's too late for screaming and begging. You move from one room to the next, without resting a minute." The rebbe stood there and he pointed to every single one of us, to Lippy, to Seymour, to Albie, to Hymie, to me too, and he pulled once more on his beard and he said, "Boys, it's a sad story. . . . You are all heading straight for Gehinnom." Then he walked outa the room and down the stairs without saying goodbye.

And you know something, I don't think he was a rebbe at all,
I think he was that angel Dumah in disguise!

That's the strangest thing what ever happened in my life
so far! That rebbe, whoever he is, scared the livin shit outa
everybody. Seymour Pinkowitz couldn't make lip farts for
two weeks after that. Even Lippy was a little shook up.
Anyway, everybody stayed in their seats until Lippy got
up and then they all went home, quick! Lippy said he
hadda go away, so I figured I'd go to the movies. Sometimes
on Sundays they don't let little kids in alone, but that's
okay, because I can pass for ten whenever I want. I comb
down my hair and I don't smile or nothin, and when I get
near the ticket booth I just stand on my toes. It works
every time! I was rich now because of the money I made on
the bubble gum. I was gonna share it all with Lippy, but
then I would hafta tell him where I got the money, and
Lippy'd break my ass. So I didn't say nothin and I went to
the movies. Abbott 'n' Costello was playing at the Dover
along with this picture called *The Phantom of the Opera,*
and I figured I needed a good laugh, so I paid out twenty
cents and I went inside. Abbott 'n' Costello aint half as good
as Laurel 'n' Hardy, but the picture was still okay. Then the
other picture came on with this guy Claude Rains and for
the first few minutes it was a real borer. But somebody
threw acid in Claude's face, and he hadda go 'round wearing
a mask, and he was always killing people at operas, that's
why they called him the Phantom of the Opera, and at the
end of the picture he gets killed and they take off his mask.
Yikes, what a face! You could die looking at it. It was all
covered with burns and marks from the acid and the skin
was all shriveled up like a dried-out lizard. That's all I

needed, two scares in one day! First Dumah and now this!
After I got outa the movie I bought two frankfurters and a
small bottle of Dr. Brown's celery tonic at the kosher deli-
catessen on the corner and then I went home. My mother
wasn't in, so I hadda go up to the roof and climb down
through the fire escape. Well, every time I eat frankfurters
I always end up on the toilet seat. I was scared to close the
door, because I figured maybe the Phantom of the Opera
was running around somewhere in one of the rooms. Maybe
he was hiding under Leo's bed right now! I was so scared
I couldn't take a crap or nothin, so I got off the toilet
seat and I tiptoed into Leo's room and I looked in all the
closets and under Leo's bed, but I couldn't find the Phantom.
Then I went into my mother's room to look for him, and this
time I grabbed Leo's baseball bat, but it was too heavy to
carry, so I hadda put it down on my mother's bed. I always
feel a little funny whenever I go into my mother's room.
Like I'm doing something wrong. So I didn't stay too long. I
just looked around for the Phantom a little and then I got
right out. I heard a big commotion going on outside in the
hall. Somebody started screaming, "Where is he, I'll kill
him!" It was Uncle Max. He came charging in and he
grabbed me by the hair. "Where's Leo!" he said, and I was a
little glad that somebody else was around, because I knew
now the Phantom wouldn't be able to get me, but it hurt like
hell the way Uncle Max was pulling my hair. Then my
mother came in, and Albie Saperstein and his uncle Bernie
the cop was with her, so Lippy and me must be up the
creek. Albie snitched about the bubble gum. Big Bernie
took over, and he told Uncle Max to let go of my hair. My
mother was crying, and that's what made me feel the worst.

Big Bernie showed me the bubble gum, and he said, "You better talk up, Benny. You're only gonna make it worse for Leo. What else did he steal?"

Uncle Max put his hands over his head, and he started shaking back and forth. "I'll have to move out from the neighborhood. I'm finished here, kaput! Who'll go into my store now except shvartzes, and gonifs like Leo. . . . I'll kill him, I'll kill him! . . ."

Well, I figured it wouldn't do no good to stall or nothin, so I went into Leo's room and I opened up the jack-in-the-box. I took out the last box of cigars, all the bubble gum that was left, and most of the silk stockings. I knew Leo would want me to save some stockings for my mother no matter what, so I left a few pairs inside. Then I brought the rest of the stuff over to Big Bernie. "That's all there is," I said.

Uncle Max stopped shaking for a minute and he looked at the stockings. "Where did he steal such merchandise, where? . . . With stockings like these I could make a fortune . . . oy!"

Big Bernie stuffed all the stockings into his pocket and he looked at the cigar box and then he put it under his arm. "Leo's in real trouble, Benny. He broke into a government warehouse. That's a federal offense. You better tell me where he is."

"A gov'ment warehouse?" I said. "Leo wouldn't do nothin like that, I know it. The F.B.I. could kill you for a thing like that, especially when it's during the war."

"You know where he is?" Big Bernie said, and then he took another look at the cigars.

"I don't know where he is, honest. I should die on the spot if I'm telling a lie!"

Uncle Max started butting in again. "Who knows? Maybe he's holding up another warehouse!"

Then Big Bernie told Uncle Max, "Come, we'll wait for him downstairs," and they left. They were gonna ambush Leo for sure. I could see my mother was in bad shape, so I said, "Ma, Leo wouldn't rob no gov'ment warehouse. He aint no crook, I don't care what anybody says. He took the stockings for you, Ma, and the cigars he got for Zaide. . . ." And then I opened up the kitchen window. My mother was so worked up she didn't know what the hell I was doing, so I just said, "I'm gonna go and help Leo." I didn't want my mother to catch a cold or nothin, so I closed the window and I went up to the roof. I knew Big Bernie and Uncle Max were waiting outside the house so I crossed over to the last roof on the block and went downstairs from there. It was beginning to rain and I didn't have no jacket, but I figured the hell with it, Leo's more important! Joe Crap's little sister Winkie was playing hopscotch in the rain with Minna Goldberg and one of the Zlotkin twins. I started jumping up and down and signaling to Winkie like a baboon, and after she did a few fancy hops and turns she finally broke up the game. "Winkie, I gotta find Leo, I gotta!" Well, Winkie don't usually give out information unless you pay up some kind of a toll, like a butt or a skate key, but she could see I was all excited so she forgot about the toll this time and she told me that Leo was up at the handball courts with Joe. "Winkie," I said, "I'll build ya a hobbyhorse when I get the time," and then I ran like a devil up to Crotona Park and around the lake where a lady got stabbed last year and up the steps that go to the handball courts. It was dark as hell, but I wasn't scared of the Phantom or nothin, I was too much in a hurry. Lippy and Joe were playing all the way over in the last court and it took me ten minutes to find 'em. A crowd of kids was standing around the court, and they wouldn't lemme get near Leo, so I just shouted out, "Leo, Leo, it's me, Benny!" and Lippy stopped the game. He looked a little worried. I guess he was losing or something. Joe Crap's supposed to be some kind of a handball champ.

"Hey, Benny, can't you see I'm playing a game?"

"You're in trouble, Lippy . . . a whole lotta trouble . . . and it's my fault. . . ."

"Stop talking like a Chinaman. What happened?"

I took Lippy over to the fence so nobody could hear us, and I told him all about the bubble gum and the F.B.I. "Lippy, you better run . . . no shit, Lippy."

"Shut up," Lippy said. "I gotta finish the game." And then he walked back to the handball court. I thought for sure the police was gonna come any minute, so I kept on the lookout for 'em, and I also watched the game. Lippy was losing pretty bad, but he wasn't gonna give up. Joe Crap's got a terrific serve, and he just kept slapping that ball down in the corner, and Leo was outa luck. Nobody can touch Joe Crapanzano's serve, nobody. Even the big guys are afraid to play him. Leo lost 21–7, and I figured he was gonna give up now, but no, he wanted to play another game. That's the way Lippy is. You gotta kill him first before you can beat him. So I said, "Leo, the F.B.I., Leo . . ." but there was nothin now I could do about it. Leo lost again. He'd kill himself to make a point, and then Joe'd come back with three. Leo wanted to play one more game, but Joe said he was pooped, so they quit. Then Leo came over to me.

"Benny, you got any money on ya?"

"Sure, I got two dollars, Lippy, here!"

"Two dollars! Who gave you all the jack?"

"Nobody gave it to me! That's the money I made from selling the bubble gum to Albie. Don't get mad, Lippy, I didn't mean nothin . . . you can kick my teeth in, but now aint the time for it. . . ."

Leo took the money and put it in his pocket, and I could see he wasn't mad at me, so I said, "Take me with you, huh Lippy? I don't care what you did. . . . If you wanna be a crook, that's okay with me. . . ."

Lippy didn't say nothin. He just put on his jacket and went through the hole in the fence. I followed him.

"Lippy . . . take me."

Leo walked to the other end of the park without saying nothin, and then he stopped and turned around. "Benny, go home!"

"Take me, Leo? . . . I won't be a pest or nothin, I swear!"

He grabbed me by the shirt and he said, "Can't you hear? Go home, you little fuck, go home. Aint you got me in enough trouble already?"

I knew it was no use asking again, so I said, "Where you gonna go, Lippy? Mommy's gonna worry if I don't tell her."

"I don't know where I'm gonna go."

"You ever gonna be back, Lippy?"

"I don't know. . . . Whatja crying for? Now go home!"

Well, I turned around and I started walking and then Leo said, "Here," and he gave me a nickel to take the bus. "You better not walk, Benny, if the boogies catch you, they'll kill you. . . . Go on, take the nickel," and then he ran like a maniac towards Third Avenue.

I didn't want Big Bernie and Uncle Max to see me, so I

went around to the other end of Seabury Place, and I
climbed over all the roofs until I got to my roof, and then I
went down the fire escape. My mother was in her room and
she didn't hear me come in or nothin. I tiptoed into the
bathroom and I wiped off my hair with a towel and then I
put on a different shirt and another pair of pants. After I was
all ready I went over to my mother's room and I knocked on
the door. "Ma, it's me, Benny, I came back." She didn't
answer me, so I opened up the door, and I could see her
sitting on her bed, and the way she was looking at me I
thought maybe she didn't recognize me. "Ma, Ma," I said,
and I was getting worried. But in a minute she was all right
again, and she said, "Benny, where did you go?"

"Don't worry, Ma, I found Leo. They aint gonna arrest
him or nothin. He's hiding out now. They can't catch Leo!"

"Benny, what did you do to me! . . . Where's Leo?"

"I don't know, Ma. . . . He didn't tell me where he was
gonna go, but don't worry, he's safe wherever he is, you
know Leo!"

Then somebody knocked on the door. It was Uncle Max
again. And right away he started in. "Henya, he didn't show
up. Somebody told him." He looked at me, and I could tell
there was gonna be trouble. "It's you. . . . You're a spy!"

"No," my mother said, "no. He was here with me all the
time, so how could he warn Leo?" Wow! My mother don't
usually tell bullshits like that. I'm the one who's always
telling lies. But I guess she figured she had enough trouble
on her hands now with Leo, and she didn't wanna get me
involved in it too. Anyway, Uncle Max was still suspicious.

"Henya," he said, "swear to me that Benny was here all
the time!"

I figured my mother was gonna back down for sure,

because she don't like to swear or nothin, even when she's telling the truth. But this time she went all the way. She swore on her life that I didn't take a step from the house, and that musta satisfied Uncle Max, because he left right away. And I was so ashamed I couldn't look her in the face. "Ma, you shouldna told a lie like that for me. . . . I aint afraid of Uncle Max."

"Shah, Benny, shah," my mother said, and I could see she was beginning to cry. There aint nobody in the whole world that's got a mother what's as good as mine, even if she gets a little crazy sometimes. That don't mean nothin. Me and Leo are still lucky to have a mother like that. I don't care what anybody says! Only thing is she picked that minute to get a little crazy, and she started copying from Uncle Max and pulling me by the hair.

"Benny . . . where is he, Benny?"

"I tol' ya, Ma, I don't know . . . I don't know . . . I don't know. . . ." I don't know what it was, but every time I said, "I don't know," she kept banging my head against the wall, hard too, so I figured it'd be better for me to shut up. And it worked, because she let go of me and she covered up her face with her hands, and she started rocking back and forth and crying out loud. And I started crying too. "Don't worry, Ma, I'll find Leo for you . . . right now!" I opened up the kitchen window again, and I started to climb out on the fire escape, but this time my mother grabbed me by the pants and pulled me back in. Then she closed the window and she said, "No more fire escapes! Uncle Max will murder you if he catches you downstairs!"

"Ma, I'll find him for you. I know all the places he could hide. . . . Lemme go find him."

"No!" she said, and I could see I better listen if I wanted to have a head left. When my mother starts swinging, she throws bombs! So I just played it safe and I stood a coupla feet away from her. "Boys I hadda be cursed with, boys!" She went into her room and closed the door. I prayed to God that Leo went someplace where he could stay outa the rain, because once he starts to sneeze he gets sick right away. And only my mother knows how to take care of him. Then I went into Leo's room. I figured maybe he'd come back, because it was raining so hard, and I was gonna wait up for him. Leo'd need a lawyer for sure, and me and him'd hafta go and look for one right away. But it'd hafta be a terrific lawyer, because it's hard as hell to win a case from the F.B.I. I stood near the window and watched the rain coming down. The way it looked the whole city was gonna be flooded. I knew it was no use waiting up, Leo wasn't coming back, not tonight. And you can think I'm a fag if you want to, but I started crying. My mother heard me. She came outa her room, and she said, "Shah, Benny, Leo will be all right." She was crying too. Then she undressed me like I was a baby or something, and she put me in my bed. And I couldn't help it, but I went right to sleep. When I got up in the morning, my mother was sitting on Leo's bed, and I could see from the way she looked that she stayed up the whole night waiting for Leo. Right away she started in on me. "Benny, get dressed, Benny, you'll be late for school!"

"I aint going to school, Ma," that's what I said, "not until Leo comes back." But I could see this was no time to mess around, so I got dressed. "Ma," I said, "Ma, you didn't call the police or nothin? . . . Because if they catch Leo, they'll give him right over to the F.B.I., and then Leo's up the creek for good. They'll put him in Sing Sing with the Crapanzano boys, Ma."

"Eat your breakfast and go to school."

"I aint hungry."

"Eat I said."

So I cut up an orange and then I had some cornflakes with milk. Meanwhile my mother put on her coat and she went down to work. There was nothin else she could do. Fox wouldn't let her take off a day no matter what happened to Leo. I got my school books and I went downstairs. I looked through Fox's window and I could see my mother sitting behind her machine like a dummy or something, her face was so white, and I said to myself, "Ma, I'll find him for you. Leave it to me." When I got to school it was still a little early, so I stood out in the yard. Ira Garfinkel was playing box ball with a new kid. Ira thinks he's something special because his father's a crummy air-raid warden and he's got a big white hat to prove it, but that don't mean nothin to me. I don't like kids that brag about their fathers all the time. Anyway, Ira and the new kid came over and Ira said, "Hiya, Benny. This is Noah. He just moved around here. His father wants to join up with the air-raid wardens, and my pop's gonna help him out." See! There aint nothin else that Ira ever talks about except his father and the air-raid wardens. And then this kid Noah says to me, "Is your father an air-raid warden too?"

"Na," Ira said. "Benny aint got no father."

"Quit foolin, Ikey. Everybody's got a father."

"Yeah, well Benny aint. You can even ask him."

So I told Noah that my father was dead.

"Your father was a soljer?"

"Yeah, it was the Japs what killed him."

"Did he get the Purple Heart?"

"Na, he didn't do nothin big. . . . He just got killed."

"Where was it he got killed?"

"I don't know. Some island."

"Was it Okinawa?"

"Na. I don't think it's got a name. . . . It was just a little island."

"Maybe it's near Manila. That's where my Uncle Mike is."

"I don't know. . . . I gotta go now. The line is going up. . . ."

It wasn't late or nothin, but I hate it when anybody starts asking me questions about my father. So I waited on line all by myself and then I went up to my class. Mrs. Krantz's my teacher and she likes me a lot. All the teachers in the school get a big kick outa me, because they can't understand how anybody who's Leo's brother can be so smart. Everybody thinks Leo's the dumbest kid in the world, that's because he never does any work. Leo aint so dumb, he just don't like school. But when it comes to doing art work, that's a different story. Even Kirschbaum the principal knows Leo's a terrific artist. If it wasn't for all the posters and signs Leo does, I think Kirschie woulda kicked him outa school long ago. Leo saves the school a fortune with all the art work he does. And Leo's teaching me how to do the posters, so I can take over for him when he graduates, if it ever happens! Anyway, Mrs. Krantz likes me and I do little posters for her all the time. Today the class was supposed to have a report ready on this crazy guy Ponce de Leon, so Mrs. Krantz told me to go to the back of the room and make up a poster quick on the Fountain of Youth, because the word was out that Kirschie was coming in to see some third-grade classes. I was worried about Leo, but I didn't wanna let Mrs. Krantz down. She depends on me a lot. So I started the poster. I made Ponce a skinny old man with a beard and a helmet, and I showed the way he was looking all over the place for the Fountain of Youth. And instead of coming out funny the way I wanted it to be, it came out a little sad. Ponce looked like an old-time rabbi from the East Side who got lost somewhere in the Bronx. I wanted to tear it up and do another one, but Mrs. Krantz wouldn't let me. She said it was a terrific job. First she hung it up near the door and then she let some of the stupid kids give their reports. She kept stalling like that because she wanted to save the best reports for Kirschie, but Kirschie never showed up. And it's a lucky thing too, because she woulda called on me for sure, and I didn't have no report ready or nothin. I was gonna do it last night, but after Leo ran away I didn't have the heart to do no homework. Anyway, when Mrs. Krantz found out it was all a false alarm and Kirschie wasn't coming, she let us out early. And I saw Albie Saperstein out in the yard. The son-of-a-bitch, he was selling Leo's bubble gum to a coupla colored kids. I caught him with the goods, so I kicked him hard in the ass, and then I took all the bubble gum away. "Bastard," I said, "why'd you go and snitch on Leo for?" Albie didn't say nothin, so I kicked him hard again. "You want me to play Gestapo with you, huh Albie? You better talk. I'll give you three. One. Two . . ."

Then Albie started bawling, maybe he thought that way a teacher would come over and help him, so I said, "Cut it,

Albie. You want me to get Joe Crapanzano after you? He'll slice off your balls with a razor."

That shook Albie up, and he stopped bawling right away, and he wiped his faggy eyes with his knuckles. Then he said, "I didn't snitch on Leo, Benny, I wouldn't do nothin like that. . . . Uncle Bernie caught me with the bubble gum and I hadda tell him. . . . I hadda, Benny, or he woulda put me in jail."

"Yeah, well maybe jail would be a whole lot better than what Lippy's gonna do to ya when he grabs ahold of ya . . . and I wanna know something, how come you still got the bubble gum, huh?"

"Uncle Bernie lemme keep a coupla pieces."

A teacher came over and I hadda let Albie go. But I didn't give him back the bubble gum. I threw it down the sewer when nobody was looking. I didn't wanna leave no evidence lying around, especially with the F.B.I. on Leo's trail. Then I started to think how it would be like to have a brother up in Sing Sing. And I made a promise to myself that I'd visit Leo every day and I'd bring him a whole stack of latkahs from my mother. But it still wasn't nice to think about, so I made up my mind not to think about nothin, and I started to walk home. But my brain's a funny thing, it kept thinking about Leo in Sing Sing, and there was nothin I could do about it. When I got to my house, the mailman was in the hall, and he gave me a postcard what was written in pencil, and it was hard to read the words because the rain got on it. But I knew it was from Leo. I can tell his handwriting any time! Leo musta bought the postcard in a candy store last night and mailed it when it was raining, that's why it was so hard to read. Well, I knew my mother'd be happy as hell to see the card, so I went right into Fox's store and I showed her the card. "Ma, Ma," I shouted out loud, and I didn't care if Fox heard me or not. "It's a postcard from Leo!"

My mother put on her glasses and she looked at the card, and then she turned it upside down and looked at it again. "Benny, now's the time for jokes? What does it say on the card? . . . It's from Leo? You didn't write it yourself?"

"It's from Leo, Ma, I swear. But it's a little hard to understand. Leo writes like a Chink. . . . I'm not lying, Ma, I wouldn't lie about a thing like that!" See! That's why it don't pay to lie. When it comes a time you're telling the truth, then people won't believe you.

"So tell me what it says on the card."

"It says . . . it says, 'Dear Ma, don't wor-ry a-bout me. Tell Ben-ny not to give you no trou-ble. I'll kill him if I find out he's making trou-ble. Leo.' . . . That's what it says, Ma, believe me!"

My mother cried a little while I was reading the card. But she wiped her eyes right away. I guess she didn't want the other women in the place to see her like that. Then she put the card away in her pocketbook, and she went back to working on her sewing machine. Fox watches his workers like a hawk, and he don't let nobody rest a minute. I saw him coming over, so I got outa there fast. And I swore to God that I'd find a job after I got outa P.S. 61, so my mother wouldn't have to work no more. I forgot to ask my mother for the key, so I hadda go up to the roof and down the fire escape. I was feeling pretty good because of Leo's card. But then I figured to myself that he wrote it last night, and who the hell knows how he was doing today! Maybe the boogies caught him and they're hiding him somewhere in Crotona Park? Maybe they put him in a sack and they drowned him in the river? Maybe they cut off one of his ears or they sold him over to Big Daddy and Big Daddy's gonna ship him off to Africa to be a slave? And I began to worry like hell. So I left a note for my mother on the kitchen table:

Mommy, I went out looking for Leo. I'll try to be back before supper. Please don't send Uncle Max or the police after me. Don't worry. Benny.

"The hell with school," I said, and then I went out the kitchen window. I almost fell off the fire escape, but I wasn't gonna let myself get killed before I found Leo. So I hopped up the fire escape, and I went back down through the roof. I figured if the boogies didn't get Leo, then he must be hiding out in the West Bronx. He'd hafta be a dope to stay around here, especially with Uncle Max and Big Bernie and the cops out looking for him. And one thing, Leo aint no dope! So I started walking towards the West Bronx. I couldn't take a bus or nothin, because I didn't have no money, and I didn't give a shit about the boogies in Crotona Park. Let 'em catch me if they want. But Monday must be a special holiday for boogies, because I passed through the middle of the park without even seeing a sign of them. But lemme tell you, when you get near Clay Avenue, there's a lotta Irish kids that hang around there, and sometimes they're worse trouble than the boogies. I was hoping to myself that the Irish kids didn't catch Leo, because they woulda killed him for sure. They hate Jewish people like poison. That's what Schwartzie says. But maybe Monday's a holiday for Irish kids too, because I walked right by Clay Avenue and over to Claremont Park without even seeing one Irish kid. But then I remembered that it wasn't three o'clock yet, and everybody was still in school, except the kids that are always playing hooky, and there's a lotta them around. I went around the whole park looking behind every bush and shouting, "Leo, chickee, it's me!"

I saw some old men hanging around the checker tables near the park house and they kept hollering and shouting like monkeys in a cage. Two old guys started in on each other and they hollered back and forth about President Roosevelt and Uncle Joe and Hitler and the war. Then one old guy said something nasty about Uncle Joe, and believe it or not, the other old guy pulled out a knife. Wow, people talk about kids being bad, these old guys were worse! They finally calmed the old guy down and he put the knife away, but he wouldn't talk to the other old guy or nothin. Then I asked the leader of the bunch if he saw Leo around, but he musta thought I was talking about a different Leo, because he started cursing me in Italian or something, and all the other old guys joined in. It was time to give up on this park, so I cursed a coupla the old guys back with some words Gran'pa taught me, then I got the hell outa there. I went down to Jerome Avenue, and I walked under the El for a little while. Leo says my father once took me and him to see a movie about Hitler with Charlie Chaplin in it, and the place where we saw it was supposed to be somewhere around here. It's called the Zenith. I had nothin else to do, so I walked along Jerome Avenue scouting for the Zenith. If I found it, maybe it'd give me some good luck, and then I'd be able to find Leo for sure. Well, I found the Zenith, but it didn't give me no good luck or nothin. I figured I better go home and eat and rest a little, and then go and look for Leo again. By the time I got to Crotona Park I was beginning to limp, and I hadda sit down. I heard a colored kid call out, "Gawd, lea' me be!" It sounded like somebody I knew. I looked over and I saw two big white kids knocking the crap outa this little colored kid. I didn't wanna mix in, but I hate to see it when somebody beats up a little kid, even if it's a boogy. So I walked over and I knew who the colored kid was right away. It was Henry Clay. He goes to P.S. 61 with me and he's only six. Why would anybody wanna beat up a little kid like that? The two white kids looked like they went to P.S. 61 too, so I said, "Hey, you fucks, leave him go, I'm Lippy's brother!" I figured they'd run away for sure after I said that, but they didn't. They left Henry Clay for a minute, and they started in on me. "Nobody's calling me a fuck!" one of the white kids said, and he knocked me all over the place. "Don't you know Lippy?" I said in a hurry. "Or Joe Crapanzano?" and I started mentioning names like crazy, even Andy Crap and Big Daddy, but it didn't do me no good. These guys didn't go to P.S. 61 or nothin. Well, one of the guys asked me if I had any money, and when I said no, the other guy punched me in the mouth. "That's for sticking up for a boogy!" It hurt like hell, but I didn't cry because I knew Lippy wouldn't like it. I just sat down on the ground and I made believe I was dead.

"You killed him, McCormick!" That's what the first guy said. They both kicked Henry Clay in the ass and then they ran away. Henry Clay was scared too. "You dead, Benny?" he kept asking me, but I didn't move until I was sure the other two guys were outa sight, and then I got up and I said to Henry Clay, "Come on, let's get outa here."

Henry Clay looked at me and he said he was glad I wasn't

dead. I told you he was a good kid. A coupla gangs of colored kids caught up with us and they asked Henry Clay who I was. "That's ma buddy Benny," Henry Clay said, so they didn't bother me or nothin. See, it pays to have a boogy for a friend! We got to the other end of the park without nobody bothering us, and I said goodbye to Henry Clay.

I met Mrs. Simonson in the street. She lives in the apartment next to us, and she said Schwartzie was very sick and my mother was up there with him. I was gonna go over to Schwartzie, but then I saw Albie Saperstein and Big Bernie coming down the block, and I figured I'd better get outa there fast. So I ran upstairs to the roof and I started climbing down the fire escape two steps at a time. When I opened up the kitchen window I heard a noise. Maybe the Phantom let Big Bernie in, so I started climbing out again, but somebody grabbed me and wouldn't lemme go. It was Gran'pa. "Benny," he said, "stop kicking." I was happy as hell, so I hugged him. "Where's Leo?" I said. "You looking for him too, Zaide?"

"Leo? He's right here!"

"What?" I said. And then I walked into Leo's room. Leo was sitting on his bed reading a Classic Comic, the son-of-a-gun! I figured to myself that he musta gone over to Gran'pa to hide, and Gran'pa brought him back. I was gonna kiss Leo, but I knew he wouldn't like it. Then I remembered about Big Bernie, so I said, "Quick, Leo, help me, we gotta barricade the door. Big Bernie's coming!" Gran'pa came into the room and I told them both what Big Bernie said about Leo robbing the warehouse.

"Warehouse?" Leo said. "Somebody's flingin around a load of crap. I didn't rob no warehouse. I got all the stuff

from a lousy candy store. Joe Crap's cousin Marco owns the
place, and I don't know where he got the loot. All I know is,
he's a bookie and a pimp, and the whole Crapanzano family
hates his guts, even Andy! And Joe said I could rob Marco
blind."

"I knew it, Lippy, I knew it. You wouldn't rob no
gov'ment warehouse. . . . But come on, hurry up, Big
Bernie's coming!"

"So let him come," Gran'pa said, and we all stood around
the door waiting for Big Bernie. Now he was gonna see how
it felt to be ambushed! This was gonna be better than the
RKO. About a minute later Big Bernie knocked on the door.
"Lemme in, Benny," he said, "I know you're in there.
Lemme in before I knock down the door." Gran'pa gave
me the signal, so I opened up. When Big Bernie saw me
and Leo standing together he musta thought he got himself
a real prize. "You're under arrest!" he said. "Both of you!"
Then Gran'pa got into the show, and I never knew it before,
but he's got more style than anybody in the whole world. He
just stood there with his arms crossed and he said, "Don't
touch those boys!" Big Bernie musta thought Gran'pa was
the chief-of-police, because right away he backed outa the
door. And then Gran'pa went to work on him. "Warehouse,
hah? Liar, bastard, skunk. Wait until I tell Captain Rabinowitz from the precinct downtown, wait! He'll fix you good.
Sonny, kiss the Bronx goodbye. It's Flatbush for you. Sure,
you took everything from the boy and then you kept it all for
yourself. Ten minutes I'm giving you to bring back everything you stole. Ten minutes and then I'm making a call to
Captain Rabinowitz." Gran'pa looked at his watch. "I'm
counting the seconds. One. Two. Three . . ."

Big Bernie's knees started to shake, and then he ran downstairs.

"Zaide," I said, "who's Captain Rabinowitz?"

"Who knows? . . . I made up a name!"

Me and Leo started counting the seconds together, and after we counted up to about one hundred and ninety-seven, Bernie came back carrying a little duffel bag. He dumped everything out on the floor and I could see he was still shivering. Leo inspected the loot, and then Gran'pa winked at me and said to Bernie, "You owe us ten cigars and three pairs of stockings. . . . Now get out!" Bernie begged Gran'pa not to tell Captain Rabinowitz and then he scrammed. His name is gonna be shit around here from now on. Gran'pa helped me put all the stuff back into the jack-in-the-box, and then Leo said, "Where's Ma?"

"Oh. I forgot, Lippy. She's by Schwartzie. She'll be here soon."

Me and Zaide and Lippy were so happy we got a little crazy, and we started dancing and singing.

Az der Rebbe Eli Melech iz gevoren zayer fraylach,
Iz gevoren zayer fraylach Eli Melech . . .

Then the door opened and my mother walked in. "Who's making so much noise?" She saw Leo and she ran over and kissed him. "Leo, Leo . . . you're not sick? You don't have a temperature? You sure, Leo? . . ." The way she was hugging him, I thought they were gonna be friends for life, but I don't know, about a minute later she started pulling his hair and everything. "Stay away all night from the house, hah! . . . How much can a person stand? . . . Oy, oy!" It's a lucky thing for Leo that Gran'pa was around,

or he woulda been finished. Gran'pa calmed her down and
then he took her into the kitchen. He started telling her
some dirty jokes in Jewish, and my mother was laughing and
everything. "Zaide, shah, . . . they'll hear you the boys."
Gran'pa knows terrific jokes about the Yeshiva student and
the rabbi's wife. My mother took out her grater and some
potatoes and she said, "Boys . . . latkahs!" And me and
Gran'pa and Leo started jumping around and singing,
"*Essen, mir gayen essen . . .*" In about ten minutes the
latkahs were ready. I was hungry as hell!

Faigele
the Idiotke

THE NAZIS WERE MARCHING ALL OVER EUROPE AND I could already see them crossing the Atlantic and capturing the Empire State Building or holding maneuvers in Central Park. "Manny," my mother kept telling me, "join up with the merchant marines or get a job in a defense plant," but I sat home. Phil was talking about going to New Orleans. We had both just finished high school and we knew that in a month or two we would be shipped off to the army. If only we'd had ten more years to live, we both solemnly agreed, we would have been the greatest painters in the world. "One month," Phil said, "gimme one month in New Orleans and then they can take me away." He wanted me to go with him,

75

but I had never been away from home even for a day and I was scared. New Orleans was like the end of the world. "Manny," Phil said, "who knows where we'll be in another three months. They'll bury us both in Africa somewhere." He was right, but I was still afraid to go. "Phil," I said, "if you want to paint, you can paint in the Bronx too." So he went by himself.

I sat home and didn't say a word to anybody and every time I heard the air-raid sirens wail I could feel my heart contract and dig all the way down to my bowels, looking for some place to hide. It was no joke. I couldn't paint or eat or anything. And then in about a week I got a letter from Phil. "Manny," he said, "it's great." And he told me stories about dark and fragrant women with melon-shaped breasts and soft, honeyed lips, and I dreamed about them day and night. Every day I got another letter from Phil with stories about even more fantastic women. "I gotta get out," I said, but I knew I could never work up enough courage to go to New Orleans.

I had to have at least one little adventure. So I stuffed three pairs of pants, some T-shirts, and a whole arsenal of paints into my duffel bag and I took out the hundred dollars that I kept in a shoe box under my bed—who could trust a bank with the Germans only three thousand miles away?— and one morning, when no one was home, I sneaked out without even leaving a note. I knew that if my mother had been home she would have been able to stop me in a minute. And then, feeling like Leif Ericson or Daniel Boone, I took the "D" train down to Delancey Street. I tried to find a room, but everywhere I went I was told that all the rooms were reserved for soldiers and sailors on leave. "Be a patriot," one woman told me, "sleep out in the street." I found a vacant telephone booth on Second Avenue and immediately called my mother. At first she laughed, but when I told her I wasn't coming back, she started to cry. "Manny, come home," she said. "No. Ma, I'm not a million miles away, I'm down near Delancey Street. I'll call you every Tuesday. . . . Ma, I have to get out . . . so send the cops after me . . . Ma, listen . . ." There was no use talking anymore, so I said a quick goodbye and hung up. It started to rain and I panicked and sat inside the telephone booth, clutching the duffel bag. A woman wanted to make a phone call, but I glared at her and finally she went away. I saw a "Rooms for Rent" sign hanging from a fire escape across the street, and I felt a little better. I opened the door of the telephone booth tentatively, popped my head out like a wily turtle, felt the rain beat harmlessly on my neck and face, and then ran across the street.

The front of the house was dark and some of the windows were boarded, but I went inside anyway. A woman with a bald spot on the back of her head and a patch over one eye met me at the door. Two black cats stood next to her with their backs humped threateningly. I almost dropped the duffel bag. Staring dumbly at her I somehow managed to communicate the fact that I wanted to rent a room. She took me up three flights of rickety stairs. The floorboards creaked, and the two black cats followed us wherever we went. I took the first room she showed me, and I figured that after I got rid of her I'd pick up my duffel bag and sneak out. She came up close to me and I thought I saw a fang mark on her neck. I would have screamed or thrown the duffel bag at her or just simply started to cry, but then she smiled a little shamefacedly and said, "Tell me, you're a Jewish boy?" I wagged my head.

"Good," she said. "I usually rent out this room for fifteen dollars but for you let it be ten." The two cats brushed against my shoes and started to purr. I felt as if I had been living in the room all my life.

"If you need any soap or towels, don't be ashamed to ask. There's a toilet on every floor but if it gets to be like Grand Central Station just come downstairs to me. Be my guest. My name is Mrs. Geller."

"Mrs. Geller," I said, "the room, is that ten dollars a week?"

"What do you think this is, the Waldorf?" She clapped her hands and smiled. "It's a lucky thing for you you're a Jewish boy. Tell me, it's the first time you're in New York? You never rented out a room before? Don't be a schlemiel, it's ten dollars a month." She started laughing to herself; the patch over her left eye moved up and down. "Sonny," she said, "be careful, or somebody'll steal off your pants." She straightened out her patch, picked up both cats, and left.

I inspected the room. The walls were chipped and cracked and the ceiling sagged miserably. There was a sink near the door with two leaky faucets. An unvarnished chest with a missing drawer and a lumpy bed with four crooked legs faced each other uneasily in one corner of the room. I killed two giant roaches and then approached the bed. I punched the mattress twice and waited eagerly for the bedbugs to appear. I turned the mattress over and punched it again. "Wait," I said to myself, "maybe they're just a little shy." I searched through my duffel bag and remembered that I had left my roll of canvas on top of the closet in my mother's room. A wrinkled shade was attached to the top of the window. I tore the shade off the window, removed one of the drawers of the chest, found a nail and four pins, and tried to stretch the shade across the back of the drawer. But the shade began to crumble, and I flung the drawer across the room. Two gigantic plaster chips fell from the ceiling and almost took out my eye. I was ready to run home.

And then I closed my eyes and had a vision of myself crawling across the ceiling of the Sistine Chapel with a paint brush in my mouth. I opened my eyes and stared at the ceiling and the walls. I felt inspired. I moved the chest over to the center of the room, loaded my pockets with tubes of paint, and climbed on top of the chest. A woman called, "Faigele, get off the fire escape." I heard a loud clank outside my window and the chest began to wobble. Pieces of plaster rained from the ceiling and struck my shoulders and the back of my head. I jumped off the chest and ran to the window. The fire escape was shaking violently and I thought the world was coming to an end.

I saw a girl who must have been at least six feet tall climb up the fire escape three steps at a time. Her skirt flared unevenly and exposed her bony kneecaps and her unwashed underwear. She stopped for a moment in front of my window and pressed her angular face against one of the panes. I stepped back. She smiled queerly and climbed up to the roof, the steps of the fire escape trembling in her wake. I took two deep breaths and went down to Mrs. Geller. I asked her for a room without a fire escape. "Shah," she told me. "It's only Faigele. She's harmless."

I was furious. "How can I get any work done with her running around like that?"

"Sonny," she said, "you'll get used to her."

"Why don't you have her arrested or something?"

"Arrested? She's only twelve years old."

Mrs. Geller's cats started arching their backs and right away I calmed down. "Well, why don't somebody tell her father?"

"Father? Her father is dead. He was killed in the war. And her mother, she works all day and when she's not working who knows where she is? So what can I do? Who else would take her in with a daughter like that? Should I throw them out in the street better? After all, Faigele's a Jewish girl. This I can guarantee." I don't know what she expected me to say, but now she was the one who was getting worked up. "Go, if you want, pack up and go. I don't care if the whole house moves out. Who needs boarders? Faigele stays! That's final!"

"All right, Mrs. Geller, all right. But could you tell her to stay away from my fire escape?"

"No! The girl goes wherever she wants." Then she backed down a little. "Sonny," she said, "you know why they call her Faigele, hah? Faigele, it means bird in Yiddish. I myself gave her that name. Why? Because she reminds me of a bird the way she runs around and hops all over. And she's kind like a bird too. The lousy kids around here they make up other names for her. But if you ask me, they're the ones who are the dopes."

She looked at me pleadingly, so I slapped my sides and said, "Let her use the fire escape, okay?" and I went up to my room. I wrote a letter to Phil and gave him my new address. "Phil," I said, "Second Avenue is not New Orleans, I know, but a little freedom is better than nothing. All I've met so far are an idiot girl and a woman with a patch over

her eye, but I've only been here for half a day." I had
nothing fantastic to tell Phil, so I made the letter short. "I'll
mail it tomorrow," I said, and using my pants for a pillow, I
went to sleep. I thought I'd have some kind of nightmare
about Faigele or Mrs. Geller's cats and I'd start screaming
in the middle of the night, but I slept soundly.

When I woke up I started to sneeze. Half my body was
covered with plaster chips. I heard somebody shout,
"Faigele, Faigele, the Idiotke," from the roof. The ceiling
began to bulge in about five or six places and I protected my
head from the bombardment of falling chips. "That's
enough," I said, and after putting on my pants, I went
up to the roof. Six kids were up there and they stood around
in a circle and all of them were shouting at Faigele. Five of
them wore black skullcaps. The other kid wore a sailor hat.
He was the ringleader and his name was Hymie. Faigele was
sitting on the tar floor of the roof with her skirt hitched up to
her knees. She was searching for her shoes. Hymie started
pumping his arms and said, "Fly, Faigele, fly!" Then the
other kids joined in, "Fly, Faigele, fly." One kid said, "Let's
play hot potata," and he tossed something up in the air that
looked like a gigantic loaf of bread or maybe a football.
Then I took a closer look. It was one of Faigele's shoes.

"Hey," I said to Hymie, "why don't you give her back
her shoe?" "No," Hymie said, "not until she flies for us."
And then the other kids joined in again. "Fly, Faigele, fly." I
tried to grab the shoe, but the kids kept tossing it over my
head and shouting, "Hold on to the hot potata." Finally one
of the kids dropped the shoe, and I snatched it up before any
of them could run over. Now Hymie called the other kids
over for a huddle. They let out some kind of a crazy cheer

and then they all separated. Faigele was still sitting on the tar floor and I wanted to warn her and give her back her shoe, but the kids started picking up dried lumps of tar and they threw them at Faigele and me. "Revenge from the Maccabees." Some of the lumps were as big as an egg. Faigele was an easy target because she was sitting on the floor, so most of the kids aimed at her. She kept getting pelted and she didn't even hide her head. I figured it was time for a little action.

I couldn't catch all six of the little bastards at one time, so I went after Hymie. He kept dodging in and out of the clotheslines, but I caught him and I gave him a good hard kick in the can. Hymie's chums had surrounded Faigele and they were getting ready to bombard her. When they saw me coming, they ran over to the next roof and started throwing tar from over there, but they were too far away to do any damage. Faigele's other shoe was still missing and I looked all over the roof for it. I couldn't find it, so I helped Faigele lace up her one shoe, and then she stood up, limped a little, and started somersaulting crazily across the roof. I guess she was performing for me. She ran nimbly along the ledge, making a noise that sounded a little like a moo. "Faigele," I said, "you'll fall off," but she didn't listen to me. Then Faigele climbed down the ladder that led to the fire escape and disappeared. I went back to my room.

About ten minutes later I heard a thumping sound in the hall, and I figured that maybe Faigele was coming up to pay me a visit. But I should have known better. She would have come through the fire escape. And like a fool I opened the door and was ready to put on a little performance of my own, when somebody grabbed me by the shirt and threw me across the room. It was Hymie's father. He couldn't have been much more than five feet tall, but his shoulders were almost as wide as the door, and, standing there with his arms dangling down almost to his knees, he looked like King Kong. I wanted to open the window and join Faigele on the fire ecape, but I was too scared to move. King Kong wore an apron that was smeared with dried blood, and I figured that he must be a butcher.

"You," he said, pointing one of his stubby fingers at me. "You like to go around kicking kids, huh?" Then he noticed a few tubes of paint that I had left on top of the chest. "A painter boy." He picked up one of the tubes, tossed it once or twice, and began to squeeze it. The cap popped off and a snaky string of cobalt blue shot out of the tube and fell with a plop on the uncarpeted floor. He seemed to be enjoying himself, and one by one he went to work on my tubes of paint. I turned around for a second and saw Faigele peering sadly through the window, and then King Kong, laughing wildly and squeezing out my last tube of paint, started coming toward me, and I must have fainted or something, because the next thing I knew, Mrs. Geller was leaning over me and slapping my face with a lumpy rag. The two black cats were climbing all over me.

"Look at him, he's turning blue. Sonny, get up!"

"I'm all right," I said, "and stop hitting me with that rag, huh?" I shooed the cats away from me and then stood up. The whole room was cluttered with lumps of paint.

"I know the whole story," Mrs. Geller said. "We'll fix him, wait. He thinks he's the boss around here, that gorilla. I'll have him dispossessed, wait. Out in the street he'll go. And Hymie, that little gangster, he'll catch it from me too."

"Thanks, Mrs. Geller, I appreciate everything, but I'm a little tired, and . . ."

"I understand, Sonny. Come down later and I'll make you some soup."

I examined myself in the mirror, but I couldn't find a bump or even a bruise. Then I heard a light tap on the window. I opened it and looked outside, but no one was around. I noticed a cracked pigeon egg and a rotten carrot on the landing of the fire escape. Presents from Faigele? The egg and the carrot stank unbearably and I wanted to close the window, but I felt that somewhere Faigele was watching me, so I cursed myself, reached out and brought the booty into the room. I wrapped the carrot and the egg in some newspaper and dropped them into the bottom of the chest.

The next morning I woke up with my nostrils stinging. The room smelled worse than a sewer. A dozen pigeon eggs, a wormy apple, and two blackened turnips were sitting out on the fire escape. "Faigele, Faigele," I cried out, but no one answered my call. I went down to Mrs. Geller. Her two cats glared at me and prepared to hump their backs, but I ignored them. "Mrs. Geller," I said, "enough is enough. Tell me where Faigele's mother lives."

Mrs. Geller stared at me for a moment, and after playing nervously with her patch, she said, "On the second floor."

"Which room?"

"The one . . . the one near the stairway. But you won't find her there. She's never home. Tell me, what happened?"

"Later," I said, "later," and I ran up to the second floor. I stood in front of the door near the stairway and knocked on it with my fist. No one was home. I sat at the top of the stairs for almost an hour, and then I went up to my room. I stuffed my nostrils with cotton, and using a rusty tablespoon I scooped the dozen eggs, the wormy apple, and the two blackened turnips into a paper bag. I went down one flight and left the bag with a little note in front of Faigele's mother's door. "The hell with it," I said, "if I stink everybody out of the house, it's Faigele's fault." I heard someone coming up the steps, and I thought it might be Faigele's mother, so I peered down the darkened stairwell and recognized King Kong. I ran up to my room.

The next morning there were no pigeon eggs or turnips outside my window, and I thought the problem of Faigele was solved. King Kong had destroyed all my Venetian red and cobalt blue, but luckily I had kept a few tubes of paint in my duffel bag. I went downstairs, scoured the block, and found several large pieces of cardboard outside an abandoned grocery store. "If Picasso can paint on cardboard," I said, "so can I!" On the way upstairs I stopped off at the second floor, but the paper bag was gone. I was eager to get back to work, and I didn't wait around to see if Faigele's mother was at home. I figured I'd try a self-portrait, so I arranged my remaining tubes of paint on the chest, posed myself in front of the mirror and started to sketch on the cardboard with a stumpy blue crayon. Then, instinctively, I turned around and saw Faigele outside on the fire escape. Mrs. Geller's two cats were with her. "Faigele's friends," I said to myself, but I kept on working. I couldn't help it, I had to turn around again. Faigele was looking at me in a funny way. She opened her mouth wide and made a sound that was somewhere between a caw and a moo, and I dropped the crayon. "Oh my God, she's serenading me," I said, and I walked over to the window and shooed her away. But Faigele stood on the fire escape and kept it up. I tried to finish the sketch, but my hand kept shaking, and Faigele's serenade froze my heart. I charged down to the second floor and beat on the door near the stairway with both fists. The door across the hall opened and Hymie came out. "Ma, Ma, look who's here!" he said, and shaking his can at me, he ran back in. Hymie's mother came over to the door. "What's the commotion?"

"I'm looking for Faigele's mother."

"Faigele's mother?"

"Mrs. Geller told me she lives on this floor. Next to the stairs."

She started laughing. "Mrs. Geller told you that? And you believed her yet? Dummy, Mrs. Geller herself is Faigele's mother!"

"What?" I said dumbly, and then Hymie's mother walked over to the door near the stairway. She just touched the knob and the door opened by itself. I looked inside. It was a storeroom. A monstrous metal crib stood near the door. A metal hoop, some gigantic wooden blocks, and a doll that was taller than I was were piled behind the crib. Faigele's old toys.

"Now you believe me or not?" Hymie's mother said.

"What about Faigele's father? Didn't he die in the war?"

She started laughing again, and I had to wait almost a minute before she calmed down. "Can she make up a story! Dummy, nobody knows who Faigele's father is—not even Mrs. Geller herself, that gypsy!"

I went down to Mrs. Geller. Her cats weren't around, and she looked lost without them. I guess she knew her little game was up.

"Mrs. Geller," I said, "why did you make up such a lie?"

She looked around desperately for her cats, and then she said, "Sonny, I'm sorry." She started to cry. "I didn't want you to move out. Who can find boarders?" A solitary tear appeared from beneath her patch and dribbled down her bumpy face. I think I was ready to cry myself, especially when I saw that tear.

"Don't cry, Mrs. Geller," I said, "I like Faigele, I mean it."

She grabbed the end of my T-shirt and started wiping her eyes with it, and I was a little embarrassed.

"Don't be angry with her, Sonny. You protected her before from those little bandits and she was trying to show her appreciation."

"It was nothing, Mrs. Geller. But please tell her not to leave any more eggs outside my window and to stay away from my fire escape. I mean, if she wants to come around once in a while, fine, but Mrs. Geller, the way it is now, I can't get any work done."

"I'll tell her, Sonny, I swear. She didn't mean no harm."

She wanted to kiss my hands, but I pulled them away quickly and put them in my pocket.

"Don't worry, Mrs. Geller," I said hastily, "who knows, maybe I'll paint Faigele's picture for you one of these days." And without giving her a chance to say anything else, I went straight up to my room. Faigele and the cats were gone, but about an hour later I had another guest. King Kong. I wasn't expecting him, so I opened the door, and he pushed his way in. He was holding some kind of petition.

"Sign it," he said.

"Sign what?"

"It's a petition to get Faigele committed. All we need is one more signature and then maybe we'll be able to get some action on it. Sign it, or I'll break your arm!"

"Go 'head." I offered him my left arm. "Break it if you want, but I'm not going to sign."

He shook his head and walked toward the door, but he changed his mind, came over to me again and started pleading. "What's the matter, aint you got any sense? The girl's an idiot. Everybody knows it, even her own mother. Look, we'll be doing Faigele a favor if we get her committed. That's a fact. Sure, if she stays around here, one of these days she'll fall off the fire escape and crack her head. I'm telling you, it's better off for everybody if Faigele goes. Mrs. Geller can't rent out a room with her around. The whole second floor is empty except for me and my wife and the kid. Everybody moved out." He took out the petition again. "Come on, sign it. Be a sport."

"No," I said flatly.

I thought he was going to pounce on me. But he waved the petition and said, "Who needs you, creep! We'll get her committed without your help. And lemme tell you, you're the next one to go." He stormed out of the room.

Two days passed. I met Mrs. Geller in the hall and told her about King Kong's petition. She looked a little worried. "You didn't sign it, no?"

"Mrs. Geller, what kind of a guy do you think I am? Sure I didn't sign." And when I told her that, she grabbed me and started hugging me and kissing me, right in the hall. Finally I made her let me go, and I went upstairs. "Sonny," she

called up to me, "now they'll never be able to take Faigele
away. I have you for an ally!"

I figured I'd continue working on the self-portrait I'd
started, so I posed myself in front of the mirror again. I
heard something drop down with a plop on my fire escape.
"Not again," I said, ready to tear out my hair. "Faigele,
Faigele, lemme have some peace." I walked over to the
window ready to scoop up turnips or eggs or whatever it
was. My fire escape was covered with tremendous lumps of
horse manure. This wasn't Faigele's doing. I mean, there's a
difference between sending somebody a rotten pigeon egg
and a lump of drek! I looked up and saw Hymie's impish face
peering over the edge of the roof. I stuck my head out the
window and, shaking my fist at Hymie, I said, "You can tell
your father that I'll never sign his lousy petition, no matter
what!" And then I realized how vulnerable I was with my
head sticking out. I closed the window quickly and was
ready to charge up to the roof, but I saw Faigele dash past
my window, and about half a minute later I heard Hymie
cry "Help, help!" I started cheering. "Hurray, hurray,
Faigele's fighting back!" I became a little frightened. Suppose she throws him off the roof? After all, it's partly my
fault. I protected her before, so now she's protecting me.
And I went up to the roof. Faigele was already gone, but
Hymie's legs were dangling out of an orange crate that was
half filled with horse manure. I laughed so hard that I had
to sit down for a minute to catch my breath. "Help, help!"
Hymie cried, and finally he managed to climb out of the
crate.

"She made you eat your own ammunition, huh Hymie?"
He walked over to the next roof without saying a word.

I bolted my door and put the chest next to it for a
barricade, and waited for King Kong to show up. I wasn't
going to take any chances. I spent half the day sitting on top
of the chest, listening, like some kind of an insane spy, for
footfalls outside my room. After a while my chin dropped
on my chest and I started to dream. Faigele and I were
playing on the roof, pretending to be birds. She kept
flapping her arms, and then, all of a sudden, she just took off
and started to fly. She flew over the roof, and I cupped my
hands over my mouth and called after her. "Faigele, Faigele,
come down. People can't fly. Come down, before you fall."
But she kept flying higher and higher. And I had to find
some way to make her come back, so I started pumping my
arms like mad, and believe it or not, here I was, flying too.
Nobody knows how wonderful it is to be able to fly. If
people could fly, I don't think they'd ever want to do anything else. I can't imagine anyone ever getting tired of flying.
My arms moved up and down effortlessly and I followed
behind Faigele. "Faigele," I said, "wait up," but I could
never catch up with her. And then my arms started feeling a
little heavy, and my body began to spin. And no matter how
hard I flapped my arms, I couldn't keep myself from falling.
But even as I plunged I thought to myself: It's worth it, just
to be able to fly for a little while. I heard somebody screaming at me. King Kong was outside my room, banging away
at the door. "Lemme in. You saw what she did to my kid,
the idiot. And you're the one who's responsible." He rammed

the door with his shoulder, but I still didn't give in. And for the first time in a long time I didn't feel guilty about not being in the army. The hell with the Germans; I had a war of my own.

"I'm telling you," King Kong said, "you better sign the petition if you wanna live to see tomorrow. . . . All right, if you're too afraid to come out, here, I'll push the petition under the door. Sign it, and then I'll go away." When the petition came through, I picked it up and tore it into a hundred pieces. With a demonic grin I sent it back piece by piece. I heard King Kong go down on his knees outside the door. He must've been trying to assemble all the pieces. I think he was crying. "Now you're gonna stay inside of that room for the rest of your life. Because if you ever try to come out, I'm gonna tear you apart. Nobody's gonna save you now. I'll be waiting for you." And then he walked down to the next floor.

Luckily I had stored seven cans of tuna fish in the bottom drawer of the chest, or I would have starved to death. Three days passed. I tried to send signals down to Mrs. Geller, but Faigele didn't come near my window, not even once. I was going to ask King Kong for a truce, but I knew it wouldn't work. I was down to my last two cans of tuna fish. And then, during the afternoon of the fourth day of the siege, I heard a knock on the door. Somebody called, "Manny, open up," and it wasn't King Kong. "Phil?" I said, pressing my ear against the door. "Is that you?"

"Who the hell do you think it is? Come on, open up."

Phil was wearing a dirty T-shirt, and he looked as if he hadn't slept for a week. I hugged him anyway, that's how glad I was to see him. I was going to tell him about Faigele and the siege and everything, but he waved me off and said, "Please, Manny, lemme rest up for a minute. I haven't been off my feet for days." I led him toward the bed. He took off his shoes and put them on the window sill. The heels and soles were worn through, and his feet were black. He wanted to fall asleep, but I wouldn't let him.

"Phil," I said, "what happened? Why'd you come back from New Orleans?" He rubbed his feet and kept quiet.

"So?" I said, and I waited eagerly for him to tell me about his adventures. But all he did was look sourly at me and rub his belly. "I'm hungry," he said. "If you won't lemme sleep, then at least gimme something to eat." So I gave Phil my last can of tuna fish. He gobbled up the whole can in less than a minute. After he licked the oil off his fingers he looked at me with his baggy eyes, and then he turned his head away.

"Manny," he said, looking at the wall, "the first day I got to New Orleans this guy and a girl caught me in back of a bar and stole my wallet and my watch. The girl wanted to take my pants and my shirt, and I hadda beg the guy to lemme keep 'em. I slept out in the street for two nights and I was even arrested for being a vagrant. Don't ask! Manny, the army couldn't be any worse than that."

"Phil, what about those letters you wrote me?"

"Ah," he said, "all lies. I thought maybe you'd come out there if I wrote you all that. It was terrible being by myself, Manny. And after a while I started believing all the crap I wrote, and I felt a whole lot better. You know. I didn't meet anybody out there. No women, nothin'."

I felt like strangling him.

"Hey Manny," Phil said, stretching his arms lazily, "wake me up after it gets dark."

And that's when I grabbed him by the ankles and threw him off the bed.

"Get out."

"What? Quit it, Manny. I'm tired. Later, huh? Then we'll play games."

"Get out!"

He put on his shoes. "You a nut, huh, Manny? First you hug me and now you wanna throw me out. All I wanted to do was stay here for one—"

I pushed him out of the room and bolted the door.

"Manny," he said, standing outside, "you turned into a madman, I mean it. Lemme in. I don't wanna go home. Manny?"

He asked me one more time before he left. I stood near the door for a minute and then I began to panic. I didn't want to stay by myself any more. "I'm sorry," I said, and I opened the door. "Phil." No one answered. I wanted to run down after him, but I was too afraid to leave my room. So I bolted the door again and sat down on the floor, and believe it or not, I started to cry. "Manny," I said to myself, "you're the king of the shmoes!" An artist I wanted to be yet!

And then, almost miraculously, I saw Faigele's face in the window. At first I thought it was only a vision, but when she started to moo I knew that it was Faigele in the flesh! "Faigele," I said, "wait, don't go away!" but she climbed up to the roof. "I'll show them," I said, and gathering up a brush, a large piece of cardboard, and some random tubes of paint, I opened the window and climbed out on the fire escape. I looked around to see if Hymie was spying on me and then I tiptoed up to the roof, gripping the metal banister tightly after every step. I looked down once and got dizzy and almost dropped a tube of paint. Faigele was playing behind a clothesline, so I walked over to her quietly, sat down on the lumpy tar floor, and placed the piece of cardboard against my knees. I watched her play for about ten minutes, and then I took out my crayon.

A pigeon landed on the roof and Faigele started to imitate the way it walked. The pigeon limped for a minute, and Faigele limped too. She smiled at the pigeon, and I stared at her, because it wasn't the smile of an idiot girl. No. Her whole face glowed and her smile was so gentle and warm that even the pigeon was baffled and stood motionless for a moment. She reached out her hand to touch the pigeon, but then she started to moo, and her features coarsened and her smile lost all of its enchantment. She was Faigele the Idiotke again, and the pigeon flapped its wings and retreated to the other end of the roof. Faigele flapped her arms too and ran after the pigeon. "Faigele, Faigele," I cried, "come back." I saw Hymie and a few of the Maccabees standing behind me and I knew King Kong would be up in a minute. I stood up, dropped the paint and the cardboard, and galloped after Faigele. The pigeon stood on the ledge of the roof. Faigele approached the ledge, flapping her arms and mooing. Hymie and the Maccabees started to shout. "Fly, Faigele, fly." The pigeon remained on the ledge for another moment and then flew off triumphantly. "Fly, Faigele, fly!" Faigele stood on the ledge and watched the pigeon, and I could see now she was crying. "Fly, Faigele, fly." She looked at me once, and then flapping her arms rhythmically, she jumped off the roof. I tried to grab one of her legs, but it was too late. Her arms flapped once or twice as her body plunged, and for a minute I thought she really was going to fly, and then her body struck the ground with a heavy thud and she lay motionless out in the yard. Mrs. Geller's cats appeared suddenly, ran over to Faigele, and started licking her body. Hymie and the Maccabees ran downstairs and I remained alone on the roof. I heard the cats begin to howl.

Even King Kong cried later when he saw Faigele out in the yard. Mrs. Geller kept beating her chest and her patch dropped all the way down and exposed the gutted socket of her eye. "I should have sent her away," she sobbed brokenly, and King Kong put his arm around her and comforted her. The two cats kept howling. I signed seven different forms, and I told the story over and over again, and finally the police left. I went up to my room and started packing. I found the pigeon egg and the carrot that I had left in the bottom drawer of the chest, and I dropped them gently into the duffel bag. And then I went downstairs.

I spent half the night wandering through the streets, bent over from the weight of the duffel bag. I kept mumbling to myself. "Let Phil be a birdman if he wants, I'm staying on the ground. I don't want to fly. Faigele, Faigele . . . I should have signed the petition." A taxicab almost ran me over and twice I was stopped by policemen. A drunken sailor offered to buy me a beer, and when I walked past him without saying a word he kicked me in the butt, and I tumbled over and fell in the gutter. The sailor picked me up and told me how sorry he was, and he made me keep his sailor hat. I peed in the middle of the street and was almost arrested, but luckily I was wearing the sailor hat and the policeman let me go. "Save it for Germany," he said with a wink. Finally I settled outside a recruiting station and sat quietly on my duffel bag. I glanced at all the recruiting posters. Uncle Sam pointed his bony finger at me and I heard him say, "Faigele, Faigele, Faigele."

The Man
Who Grew
Younger

Bernstein, the translator, warily climbed the first of the forty-nine steps that led to Misha's room: he was on the lookout for spiders and rats. He stopped after the twenty-fifth step and removed a lumpy handkerchief from his vest pocket. "Misha, Misha," he mumbled plaintively to himself, and, holding his swollen hand against his chest, he checked his heartbeat. A long furrow appeared at the back of his bald head. Bernstein was convinced that he was going to die before he reached the forty-ninth step. He cursed himself for associating with publishers and poets. And he petitioned the devil to destroy the stairway.

He knocked timidly on Misha's door. Bernstein was not worried. He knew that if he waited long enough Misha

would let him in. And so, to while away the time, he started
talking to himself. He hurled prolific curses at Misha, and
Popkin the publisher, and then cursed himself for not being
a haberdasher. He envisioned himself boiling Misha and
Popkin, Pushkin and Peretz, Gogol and Sholem Aleichem in
a huge blackened pot. The door opened suddenly, and
Misha's bloodless face startled Bernstein. His untrimmed
mustache and deeply cloven chin reminded Bernstein of
some sinister Jack of Spades he had once seen in a deck of
hand-painted cards belonging to a one-eyed Armenian.

"So?" Bernstein said. "Are you letting me in or not?" and
then he shuffled past Misha. Six or seven black penholders
stood in a cracked jar on the desk near the door. A bottle of
ink with a rubber plug and a single penpoint were stationed
near the jar. A notebook with irregularly-lined paper sat on a
narrow bench behind the desk. Bernstein hovered around
Misha's steam pipe and slowly warmed his hands. Near the
steam pipe was a toilet with a chipped seat and a huge
wooden basin that Misha used for a bathtub. Bernstein's jaw
dropped suddenly and he moved away from the steam pipe.
"Bandit," he called out, and he chased a cockroach across
the room. Misha removed the plug from the ink bottle and
selected a penholder. The cockroach eluded Bernstein, and
he sat on the toilet seat and brooded for a moment. The
sound of Misha's pen scratching the notebook paper roused
him, and he placed his elbows on his knees and rocked back
and forth on the toilet seat. He waited for Misha's pen to
stop moving, but the scratching sound continued. "Misha, I
talked again to Popkin. Misha . . ."

He clapped his knees together. "Misha, I'm sixty-seven
years old. Can I go out now and look for a job?" He
complained to the steam pipe. "A chance comes along once in

a lifetime and he says no!" Then he stared darkly at Misha and started rocking again. "Sure, you can afford to be particular. You at least have Rosalie the Widow to look after you. But not everyone can be a poet. I don't have a widow to wash for me my underwear. After all . . . Misha!"

Misha's stooped back shielded him from Bernstein's onslaught, and he continued to lean over the desk and write. Bernstein decided to attack him from another position. He was not desperate; he know that Misha was vulnerable. So he stood up and walked around the desk. Misha's face hardened, but the hand that held the pen trembled slightly. Bernstein gripped the edge of the desk and glared at Misha. The penholders rattled in the cracked jar.

"Forty years I worked with you, Misha. Forty years. I was for you an agent, a friend, a translator, a father!" He held out the swollen fingers of his left hand. "For five years I went to night school just to learn English so I could translate for you your stories and your poems. You remember, Misha, how I would run over to Henry Street in the snow or in the rain without galoshes or a scarf or a coat, and with my grammar book under my shirt, so it shouldn't get wet. I did it for me, Misha, eh? For me! Sure, when they saw you sitting in Rattner's or the Royale, everybody said, 'Misha Dubrinoff, the Yiddish Lermontov!' And they all laughed at me. They saw me with my grammar book, and they called me *Yeshiva bucher.* After all, who needed Broadway when you had Second Avenue? And I warned you, and Shmulka, and Boris. Wait, I said, wait. In ten years everybody will move away from Delancey Street and then only the bedbugs and the lice will have the time to read your poems and your plays. So I wasn't a hundred percent right. It took thirty years instead of ten! Misha . . ."

Misha placed his pen on the table and closed the ink bottle. Bernstein pressed his perspiring face closer to him. "For twenty years I'm running after Popkin. 'Popkin,' I tell him, 'I know you publish books only in English. Who can blame you? After all, you're a businessman. So let me, I'll translate five or ten of Misha's stories, put them in a book, and I give you my personal guarantee that I will sell for you myself ten thousand copies. What, Misha is the king of Delancey Street. They worship him!' 'No,' he says, 'no. Who needs Yiddish poets!' 'Popkin, with my translation he'll be another Shakespeare.' 'One Shakespeare,' he says, 'is enough.' So I send him letters, and notes, and telegrams, I call him on the telephone three times every week, I curse him, I threaten him, but it does me no good. They see me come near his office and they lock the doors. He threatens yet to call the police. And then, all of a sudden, everybody is reading Peretz and Bashevis Singer, and it becomes fashionable to print Yiddish poets, and now he's the one who sends telegrams and notes. Misha, I know, I know he's a low life, but a publisher is a publisher!"

Bernstein produced three crumpled letters from his vest pocket. "Here, Misha, read for yourself." He placed the letters one at a time on the table. Misha walked away from the table and stood near the toilet seat. Bernstein's temples pounded; he expected a heart attack or a stroke. He clasped his hands and calmed himself. "Misha. Do I have to walk around for the rest of my life with one suit to my name? Misha, do it, do it for me!" He shuffled blindly toward the toilet seat, banging his shoulder against the steam pipe. "Misha, if not for you I could have become a haberdasher, like my sister's husband. With my own store and everything.

But I stuck instead with you. . . ." Bernstein watched Misha's shoulders slump, and he continued his attack. "Sure, I could have married Fritzie, the baker's daughter, and by now I would be living in Riverdale with two Buicks and a Siamese cat. But who needs Riverdale? Misha, I'm asking from you something so terrible? . . . I'm trying to help you! With Popkin, who knows, you could even win a Pulitzer Prize! Give me the green light. Misha, yes?"

"No."

Bernstein checked his heartbeat hastily and dropped down on the toilet seat. He was trying to regroup his forces for another attack. He stalled for a moment. "So give me at least a reason."

"I don't have to give out reasons. No is no."

"Misha. One reason."

The cleft in Misha's chin deepened and his nostrils flared.

"If Popkin wants me, let him publish the stories I'm writing now, not the stories I wrote thirty years ago."

"Misha, who can understand the stories you're writing now? I mean it! Now you write riddles, not stories. Cows that talk in ten languages, men who grow younger instead of older, women who go around naked day and night. Can you blame Popkin if he doesn't like them? You don't even bother to write sentences any more! Misha, honest to God, last week it took me three days to translate one line. I don't understand the stories in Yiddish, so how can I write them over in English?"

"Then let Popkin hire another translator!"

Bernstein stared dumbly at the steampipe and mumbled to himself. "For forty years I work for him and now he says Popkin should find another translator." He closed his eyes

and rocked back and forth on the toilet seat with a demonic
half-broken rhythm; the hinges began to creak. One of the
penholders fell out of the jar and rolled toward the edge of
the table. Bernstein quieted the toilet seat and shamefully
opened one eye. Misha placed a package in his lap. Bernstein's fingers clutched the package incredulously.

"Go already!" Misha said. "Burn together with Popkin."

Bernstein tried to mask his emotion. "Misha, are you sure
you didn't leave out any of the old stories. Popkin wants all
of them."

Misha lifted Bernstein off the toilet seat and carried him
toward the door. Bernstein, cradled in Misha's arms, held
the package against his chest. Misha put him down near the
door.

"Bernstein, I never asked you to be my translator."

"I know," Bernstein said wistfully, "that's my fate."

Misha pushed him outside the door. "Misha, you won't
regret it. You'll see. Stick with me, Misha, and you'll never
go wrong." The door closed, but Bernstein kept talking.
Then he paused and knocked on the door with one finger.
"Misha?" He knocked again. "Misha? . . . Don't worry.
Leave everything to me. I'll make sure that Popkin takes the
story about the man who grows younger. I'll finish translat-
ing it tonight."

Bernstein gripped the banister with his left hand. And for
the first time in his life the forty-nine steps did not gall
him.

"Misha, Misha, Misha."

Rosalie the Widow stacked the empty Pepsi-Cola bottles
in even rows near the steam pipe, and then, with one sweeping motion, dusted and washed Misha's toilet seat. Rosalie's

washcloth was ubiquitous. Misha retreated behind his desk; he was in no mood to have his ears and his armpits scrubbed.

Rosalie cursed him. "Pig." Misha eyed her washcloth and remained behind his desk. She removed his books from the floor, dusted them, and paying no attention whatsoever to author or title, she arranged them on the shelf that her own brother, Itzie, had made for Misha. Misha despised the shelf. But he knew that if the shelf disappeared his life would be in danger. Itzie Himmelfarb was the sheriff of Delancey Street. When Bilka Bendelson terrorized the entire East Side thirty years ago, Itzie organized every butcher from Ludlow Street to East Broadway. And one day in June Itzie and his butcher army marched on Bilka's Second Avenue headquarters, and drove Bilka and his stooges out of the East Side for good.

Rosalie put her washcloth on top of the shelf, and for the first time Misha allowed himself to relax, and even dared to light a cigarette.

"Misha," Rosalie said, "so?"

Misha pretended that he was working. But he knew that there was no real way of avoiding her.

"How long will I have to remain a widow?"

Rosalie picked up her washcloth again, and Misha dropped his cigarette.

"Misha," she said, "Itzie wants an answer. Five years is time enough. . . . Misha, remember, I have property."

"I know."

"Five offers I had last week. Five. Everybody wants to marry me. Misha, honest to God, Rabbi Gershenson is ready to divorce his wife."

Misha laughed for Rosalie's sake.

"Misha, how long can I wait? Give me already an answer. Yes or no."

Misha tried to avoid both Scylla and Charybdis. "No," and Itzie would be up in a minute and throw him off the roof. "Yes," and he would have to put up with Rosalie's washcloth day and night in this world and the next. But the constant agony of "maybe" was becoming for Misha a fate worse than Scylla and Charybdis combined.

"Misha," Rosalie said, "yes or no."

Misha glared at the Pepsi-Cola bottles stacked near the steam pipe. "No," he said, first to himself, and then to Rosalie. He had to tell her again before she would believe him. She folded her washcloth.

"Wait," she said, "wait. Leads a widow on for five years. Wait. You expect Itzie to stand around while his sister is disgraced? . . . Misha, I'm thinking now only of you. Maybe you should reconsider."

The cleft in Misha's chin deepened, and Rosalie knew that Misha's "no" was final. She felt a pain in her chest and started to cry. "Bum, bastard," she said. "A poet I had to pick! Itzie warned me not to wait around. He'll knock nails in your head for what you did to me. Nails."

From Misha's desk she stole the aluminum lamp with the retractable neck that she had given to him for his fifty-seventh birthday. She tore the lamp's shade and broke the retractable neck, and after depositing the remnants of the lamp on top of the shelf she sneezed and left.

The broken neck of the lamp kept swinging jauntily over the sides of the shelf and seemed to perform for Misha. He knew that it would be useless to hide or barricade the door, and so he sat and waited for Itzie. After searching through the shelf he found a battered copy of Sholem Aleichem's stories, and sitting at his desk, he began to read.

When Misha heard the doorknob rattle he put down the book. His knees were knocking, and he chided himself for being afraid. For a moment he even wished that he had stalled Rosalie at least a little while longer. He might have packed his books and moved uptown. But no matter where he had gone—Parkchester, Scarsdale, or Tel Aviv—Himmelfarb would have found him in the end. He smiled philosophically to himself and waited for Itzie to break down the door. The doorknob stopped rattling. Faintly, almost inaudibly, he heard someone call his name. He knew who was standing outside his room.

Bernstein kept wheezing. "Who can climb steps any more?" Misha unbuttoned the collar of Bernstein's shirt, brought him a glass of cognac, and then bolted the door. Bernstein was crying.

"Misha," he said, "Popkin refused us." He sought Misha's toilet seat. "Refused us. 'Popkin,' I said, 'take ten of the old and one of the new.' 'No,' he says. He changed his mind. He's no longer interested in Yiddish writers. Just like a whore. Now Mexican poets are in fashion. Misha, I begged him. 'Popkin, Popkin, take "The Man Who Grew Younger," you can't go wrong. Let ten years go by and it will be a classic. Popkin, I'm giving you my guarantee.' Classics he doesn't need. Only Mexican writers." He stumbled across the room, narrowly missing the steam pipe and the Pepsi-Cola bottles, and finally found the toilet seat. "Misha, are you listening to me or not?"

"What, what?"

"The deal with Popkin is off. We can't even worm from

him a cent. You, you're a lucky man. You still have Rosalie."

Misha's lips shaped an ironic smile. "No more Rosalie. I packed her in."

Bernstein rocked his head in disbelief. "Misha, you gave up a gold mine. The woman is worth a fortune. Gershenson told me himself. He knows her finances. . . . Is this a Misha! Worse than a child. Misha, I mean it, without me you would be lost altogether. Forget about Rosalie! How will you handle Himmelfarb?" Bernstein, absorbed in Misha's sorrows, sucked his lip. "Misha, I have a plan. I'll take Rosalie off your hands. Sure, for you I'll make the sacrifice. You think that will satisfy Itzie, hah?" He drew his knees together and answered his own question. "What's the use, a *zhlub* like that, he'll fracture your head together with mine."

Bernstein clutched his chest; his lips turned ashen and his eyebrows twitched. Misha strode across the room and gripped Bernstein's hand. Then he stooped, lifted Bernstein gently, and brought him over to the bed. Bernstein's eyebrows stopped twitching. Misha covered him with a blanket. "See," Bernstein said, raising his chest wearily, "see. If it's not the heart then it's the liver. Misha, maybe I should go home?"

"Stay."

"So where will you sleep?"

"What, the bed is not big enough for two?"

"Misha, you know me. I snore. And I talk all the time when I sleep. Misha, I'll rest here for a little while and then I'll go."

"Bernstein, you have to make such a big production out of staying in a bed. Do, do whatever you want. But remember, you won't find an escalator outside my door.

Bernstein envisioned himself tumbling down Misha's forty-nine steps, and his lips turned ashen again. "Misha, maybe you're right. I'll stay here tonight. Misha, why are you standing by the door? Are you expecting somebody?"

"I'm expecting Itzie."

"Itzie," Bernstein said, "I almost forgot." He pulled away the blanket. "Misha, let's stay better at my place."

"My place, your place. He'll find me just the same."

"Misha, maybe we should go to Mexico? I mean it."

Misha covered Bernstein again. "Go, sleep. You give me headaches with your speeches."

Bernstein sat glumly for a moment.

"Misha—"

"What?"

"Don't worry about Itzie. I'll talk to him. Itzie listens to me. 'Itzie,' I'll tell him, 'What's fair is fair. There's no obligation on Misha's part. Where's the contract? The rabbi was never called in. Misha never promised to marry her. But it's his misfortune. Rosalie is a jewel. And she has bonds yet and two houses in Brownsville. Itzie, believe me, Rosalie is better off. Misha's no bargain. The man never worked a day in his life. Let him *drai* someone else's *kop* with his poetry.' Misha, what do you think? He'll listen to me or not?"

Misha stood near the steam pipe. Bernstein kept counseling Itzie, Misha, and himself. "You'll see. All right, I'm not the Baal Shem, but I know how to talk. And if Itzie brings Rosalie with him, I'll take her over to the toilet seat and talk to her privately. 'Rosalie,' I'll say, 'live and laugh. You should be glad he's giving you your release. . . .'"

"Go to sleep."

Bernstein hid under the blanket.

"Misha?"

Misha raised his arms despairingly.

"What does he say, your man, your man who grows younger all the time? *'The world is a shithouse.'* The man is a lunatic, but honest to God, he's a hundred percent right. A shithouse!" Bernstein clapped his knees. "Nobody, not Chekhov, not Tolstoy, not Babel, not Gogol, not Sholem Aleichem, nobody writes a story like Misha Dubrinoff."

Bernstein's chin dropped onto his sunken chest. He slept quietly.

Misha kept vigil near the toilet seat.

"Bastards," Bernstein cried out in his sleep, "bastards. Popkin, listen to me!"

Misha approached the bed. He gripped Bernstein's hand.

Bernstein opened one eye. "Misha, did he come yet, the *zhlub?*"

"No."

"Don't worry, Misha. I know how to handle him. Don't worry. You'll see. Itzie listens to me. Misha, should I run home and get my balalaika? My balalaika could bring over the devil to our side. Misha, you know it. Misha, you think he'll come? Maybe we should both run over to the precinct. There we'll be safe. Misha, maybe he won't come. Maybe Rosalie forgot to tell him. Misha, what do you think?"

"He'll be here. If not now, then later. If not today, then tomorrow. This I can guarantee."

Bernstein humped his back. "So what can we do? We'll wait for him."

They sat in the dark. Bernstein cursed Itzie and Popkin. Misha watched the door.

Imberman

FATHER ZAMOYSKI WAS SUPPOSED TO BE IN CHARGE OF
the weightlifting club, but he couldn't even measure Billy
Wisnoiwiecki's biceps, and every time we wanted to work out
we had to climb up the steps of the rectory and wait until he
found his keys. He gave us three dumbbells and a bench and
let us use one of the storerooms, but the storeroom was worse
than Billy Wisnoiwiecki's cellar. I didn't mind the cockroaches and the ladybugs, but the ceiling leaked and we
couldn't walk into the storeroom without wearing our galoshes. Billy Wisnoiwiecki complained all the time, and he
told everybody that he was going to quit the club and join
the Crotona Y. "That's right," he said. "I'd rather work out

113

with the Yids." And one day, while we were walking over to the rectory to get Father Zamoyski's keys, Billy grabbed my hand. "Come on, Sig, let's go over to Yiddeltown and grab a workout." We stopped off at Billy's house. "Wait here," he said, and he went inside for a minute. He came out holding two paper party hats.

"What's that for?"

"It's a *yamkah*. All the Yids wear them. They won't let us in without one."

And while we walked across Crotona Park, Billy kept coaching me.

"Remember, you gotta act like a Yid."

"How?" I said. "How?"

"Just wear your yamkah, and let me do most of the talking. And don't tell anybody you take baths."

My father had told me that the Crotona Y was a hangout for pimps and dope peddlers, and that if they ever caught a Catholic boy inside, they would shave his head and make him eat worms. Of course I never really believed him, but still, when we came to the other side of the park, I was scared. I mumbled an act of contrition and clutched the Holy Name medal inside my shirt. Billy gave me one of the party hats.

"What are you waiting for?" he said. "Put it on."

The huge Star of David over the door of the Y seemed to portend my doom, and I wanted to get rid of my party hat and run. Billy pushed me through the door. "You better behave," he whispered, pinching my arm, "or we'll both be screwed." He approached a man sitting glumly behind a desk. "Which way to the weightlifting room, huh Pop?"

"Where's your card?"

Billy faltered for a moment. Then he said, "We aint got no card. We're visitors." He pointed to his party hat. "From the Jennings Street Yeshiva."

The man removed two cards from a drawer. "What's your name?"

"Hymie Wasserman."

"And him?"

"Benny Finkenberg. Just put down Fink for short."

The man gave us our cards and told us that the weightlifting room was on the fourth floor. Billy pulled me toward the stairway. "We're in," he said, and he started laughing to himself. "What a name I picked out for you, Siggy. Finkenberg. The Fink." Billy laughed all the way up to the third floor, and then we felt the banister shake, and I thought that we were both going to fall down the stairwell. I heard someone shout, "Imberman, do you have to do squats with four hundred pounds?" Billy gripped the wall with both hands and crouched toward the fourth floor. The yamkah had fallen off my head. I picked it up and followed Billy. We entered a room that was almost as small as Father Zamoyski's storeroom. The floor was covered with a thick, bumpy mat that was beginning to shred. Barbells and dumbbells, peanut shells and cherry pits, huge metal plates and battered Indian clubs cluttered the mat. Near the door was a leg-pressing machine with greased bars, a "lat" machine with a curved handle and a wire pulley, and a squat rack with two crooked stanchions. Three inclined benches leaned against the rear wall, and each bench could be lowered and raised by turning a handle. There were half a dozen weightlifters in the room; all of them were older than Billy and I, and not one of them wore a yamkah. Five of the weightlifters were bunched around a huge mirror that lined one of the side walls. They all had their shirts off, and they took turns strutting in front of the mirror. Billy stared at them. I was unimpressed. While Billy inched reverently toward the mirror, I inspected the lat machine and the inclined benches, and watched the other weightlifter, the only one in the room who was actually working out. He was an inch or so taller than I, and he had tremendous ears, and hair that was flecked with sawdust and dandruff and matted with grease. He wore a flannel sweatshirt that reached his knees, and a pair of battered sneakers that were unable to accommodate his toes—they stuck out like ten defiant little men. He stood near the squat rack and stared intently at the ceiling. Then he stooped and brought his head and shoulders under the barbell that rested on the squat rack. Ten enormous metal plates were stacked at each end of the barbell. He breathed deeply and lifted the barbell off the rack. One of the weightlifters near the mirror slapped his thigh. "Everybody, run for cover," he said, "Imberman is squatting again."

The mirror began to rattle, and the Indian clubs hopped all over the mat. I tripped and fell over the lat machine. The wire pulley wrapped itself around my leg. Billy hid under one of the inclined benches. The weightlifters laughed and booed and hurled peanut shells at Imberman. "Throw him out." Imberman squatted with the barbell on his shoulders and then returned the barbell to the rack. One of the weightlifters saw Billy hiding under the inclined bench. Billy pointed to his yamkah and stayed under the bench. "Hymie Wasserman," he said, "from Jennings Street. And that's the Fink over there. We want to join up."

"All right," the weightlifter said. "Take off your shirts. I'm Harvey Rosen, the instructor. You can call me Biceps."

Harvey Rosen was over six feet tall. He probably had the biggest biceps in the world. All the time he was talking to Billy, he kept peeking at his biceps in the mirror. He must have been the king of the Crotona Y, because the other weightlifters left half the mirror free for him. And no matter where Harvey Rosen stood in the weightlifting room, his rights to the mirror were unchallenged. He put on a little show for Billy. He wiggled his left arm, and told Billy that he could make his biceps dance the mambo. "Jesus," Billy said. I watched Imberman do leg presses.

Billy followed Harvey Rosen all over the weightlifting room. I took off my shirt and picked up two Indian clubs. Billy ran over to me. He looked a little frantic. "Siggy, you crazy! Put your shirt back on. Your medal is showing. The Yids'll bury both of us if they see it." I put the medal in my pocket and Billy went back to Harvey Rosen. Imberman began doing squats again.

Harvey Rosen cupped his hands over his mouth and said, "Imberman, you bum, go home."

"Yeah," Billy said, "go home." He seemed very satisfied with himself.

This time I stayed away from the lat machine. And while the mirror rattled and the Indian clubs hopped, I held on to one of the inclined benches. When Imberman finished squatting, Billy came over to me again. "Come on, Sig. Let's go. I'm getting tired of wearing a yamkah and talking like a Yid."

I thought about the lat machine and Imberman's toeless

sneakers while we walked back across Crotona Park. Billy kept congratulating himself. "What a stunt I pulled off, huh Sig?" He crushed his party hat, turned around and hurled it in the direction of the Y. "We fooled all the Yids." Then he started talking about Imberman. "The guy eats garbage, Sig. I swear it."

"Who told you that?"

"Biceps. Biceps Harvey. He says Imberman works out every day. He wears that sweatshirt all the time. And he eats garbage."

When we came to Billy's house, I told him that I was going to join the Y.

"Are you crazy? I mean, once is okay. But who wants to work out with Yids three times a week? And you think I want people to call me Hymie Wasserman for the rest of my life? Come on, we'll make Father buy us a new bench and some more dumbbells.

"No," I said, "I'm gonna join the Y."

I signed my membership card Sigmund Dombrowski, and nobody bothered me. I wore my medal and told Harvey Rosen that my name wasn't Finkenberg, and that I wasn't Jewish. He said that half the weightlifters at the Y weren't Jewish, but I could see he was a little disappointed that Billy wasn't with me. I didn't worship his biceps and I wouldn't laugh when he mimicked Imberman doing squats. After my second or third workout he lost all interest in me and didn't even bother giving me a program.

I copied all of Imberman's exercises. When Imberman did bench presses, I did bench presses. And when Imberman did lateral raises with two thirty-pound dumbbells, I grabbed a pair of Indian clubs and followed suit. Harvey Rosen called me Stooge, Fink, and Polack, but I still worked out with Imberman. And soon all the other weightlifters started throwing peanut shells at me too. I thought of barricading myself behind the squat rack and flinging Indian clubs and sawdust at Harvey Rosen and his chums, but the catcalls and the peanut shells never bothered Imberman, and I gave up the idea of a barricade.

Imberman never liked to talk very much, so we just worked out. But once while we were resting, I asked him why he worked out, and he told me that working out with weights was like playing a game. Only it was much better than football or pinochle or even chess, because he didn't need teams or partners or anything. The weights were his only opponent, and they never cheated or threw cherry pits. The barbell on the squat rack had no hidden snares or devilish tricks. It merely exerted four hundred pounds of resistance that he had to overcome. And the stronger he became, the more plates he would stack at both ends of the barbell, and he would pit himself against a more powerful opponent. I asked Imberman if he had any friends. He said no. I was still curious about him, but I didn't want him to think I was prying. So we continued working out in silence.

My mother usually made me peanut butter sandwiches after school, and I would bring them with me to the Y. I told her that I was very hungry after I finished working out, and she gave me extra food. Most of it went to Imberman. Once my mother brought home some sandwiches from my cousin Wally's confirmation, and I packed the sandwiches and two pineapples in a shopping bag and brought everything over to the Y. I figured that now Imberman would have enough food for a week. But Harvey Rosen stole the shopping bag and distributed my sandwiches to all the weightlifters. He kept the two pineapples for himself. I tried to grab the shopping bag away from him, but he picked me up and put me on top of the leg-pressing machine. Then he bowed and called me King Shit. Imberman saw me sitting on top of the leg-pressing machine and told Harvey Rosen to take me off.

"Don't start up with me, Imberman," Harvey Rosen said. "I'm the instructor here, not you."

Imberman picked up a seventy-five-pound dumbbell.

Harvey Rosen stared at the dumbbell for a moment and then took me off the leg-pressing machine. My neck and shoulders were covered with grease. Imberman put down the dumbbell.

"You try that again, Imberman, and you're through here," Harvey Rosen said. He walked over to the mirror and started juggling the two pineapples. The other weightlifters cheered him.

Imberman laced his sneakers and walked out of the weightlifting room. "Imberman," I called, "wait for me."

Imberman was the janitor of an old building on Washington Avenue. He lived in the basement. His father died during the war, and his mother moved to California with a jewelry salesman. He was seventeen, but with his pinched, goblinlike face he looked about thirty. He quit school when he was thirteen, and ran off to Florida for a year. He had lived in Baltimore and Kansas City and New Orleans, and had even thought of visiting his mother in California. He stole a car when he was fifteen, and spent six months in a two-room jail in Georgia. When the jailor found out that

Imberman was Jewish, he beat him over the head with a belt
buckle and made him eat swill for a week. After he was let
out of jail, he picked oranges for a little while and then came
back to New York.

I helped Imberman run the dumbwaiter and take out the
garbage cans, and then we went down to his room in the
basement. The room had a lumpy cot, a barbell, and a lone
toilet. From under the cot Imberman removed a chunk of
halvah that was wrapped in toilet paper. The halvah was
pocked with holes and crumbled even before I touched it,
but I ate a piece anyway. Imberman asked me if I wanted to
meet a Puerto Rican whore who lived in the next building.
He knew her personally, he said, and I could "ride" on her
for free. I told him that I was only twelve. He smiled, and
looked more like a goblin than ever. I told him that I would
meet him at the Y in two days.

My father found out I had joined the Y and was furious.
He told me that if I ever went near the Y again he would
lock me in the cellar for a week. And so I forgot about
Imberman and Harvey Rosen and the lat machine, and
retreated to Father Zamoyski's storeroom. Billy Wisnoiwiecki was now the boss of the weightlifting club. A mirror
was attached to the back of the door and Billy looked at his
biceps all the time. He had calked the holes in the ceiling
and had soldered all the broken seams in the steam pipe.
He built an inclined bench from two orange crates and an
old ironing board, and took a broomstick and some rope and
made a primitive lat machine. At first Billy called me The
Yid and wouldn't let anybody talk to me. But I was the only
one who could lift the barbell, and Billy broke down after a

while and told me that I could be his weightlifting partner. I didn't enjoy working out with Billy, because after every exercise he would run over to the mirror and inspect his biceps. And every time I sat on Billy's inclined bench or gripped the handle of his lat machine, I thought about Imberman and the Crotona Y.

One day after school I bought a dozen oranges and a pound of halvah from Jennings Street and went looking for Imberman. I didn't want to disobey my father's injunction, so I bypassed the Y and walked over to Washington Avenue. The windows of Imberman's building were boarded up and I knew that the building had been condemned. The garbage cans were stacked in crooked rows near the cellar entrance and were filled with cinders. I said a "Hail Mary" and a "Glory Be" and went over to the Y. Imberman's barbell wasn't on the squat rack. Harvey Rosen was at a meeting, but one of the other weightlifters told me that Imberman had been banned from the Y. "Yeah," he said, "Imberman was doing squats with five hundred pounds, and he tripped over a peanut shell or something, and his barbell fell through the floor. So Biceps banished him. I mean, the whole building almost collapsed." I left the oranges near the lat machine. "For Harvey," I said. I saved the halvah.

Billy Wisnoiwiecki went to Clinton and played on the football team. In his sophomore year he made All City and talked about going to Notre Dame. I went to Bronx Science. I still worked out with Billy every Tuesday and Thursday night. Billy would strut across the storeroom wearing his Clinton sweatshirt, and he talked about all the girls from Freeman Street that he was going to lay. "I'd bring 'em over to the storeroom," he told everybody, "but I don't want to get Father into trouble." I had at least two hours of homework every night, and sometimes when I worked out I brought along my French grammar book and studied the subjunctive or the passive voice. Steve Reeves had won the Mr. America contest the year before, and Billy had pictures of him tacked on every wall. One Thursday Billy charged into the storeroom like a wildman. "Come on, Siggy, put on your coat."

He dragged me out before I had time to button my pants. "Where the hell are we going?"

"To the Mr. New York City Contest. I just got the word. Steve Reeves is gonna be there."

So we rode downtown and waited on line for an hour outside the Roosevelt auditorium. Billy kept fidgeting in his seat and didn't even watch the contest. "Where's Steve Reeves?" I lost all interest after the third or fourth muscle man paraded across the platform. Harvey Rosen was one of the contestants, and when he posed on the platform I gave him a rousing boo and enjoyed myself for the first time. Billy told me to shut up. Harvey didn't win the contest, but he won the "Best Biceps" award. Billy was ready to tear down the pillars of the auditorium. "Where the hell is Steve Reeves!" And then the announcer climbed the platform, tightened the neck of his microphone, and said, "Ladies and Gents, now we have for you the special event of the evening." Billy gripped the armrests of his chair and shook them. The curtain was drawn. A barbell with fifteen plates at each end rested on a squat rack with gleaming metal stanchions. "Oh, my God," I said. The announcer jabbed his finger in the direction of the barbell, and said, "Ladies and

Gents, tonight . . . here . . . before your very eyes . . . you will witness . . . a new world's record . . . Marvin Imberman . . . formerly of the Crotona Y . . . and presently unattached . . . will attempt . . . to perform a squat . . . with *sev*-en *hun*-dred pounds . . . on his shoulders."

"Marvin Imberman," I mumbled to myself "Marvin Imberman." No one had ever used his first name before. "Imberman" always seemed final, complete, almost magical. Like Samson or Beelzebub. "Imberman" could do anything. Squat with seven hundred pounds in a wink. But "Marvin Imberman" was another story. I stared at the gleaming stanchions and sensed disaster.

Billy tugged my arm, but I wouldn't move. "What a fraud. They send the word around that Steve Reeves is coming. And look what shows up!"

He left without me.

The lights in the auditorium were dimmed one at a time. Only the intense light above the platform was left on. Imberman appeared. He was wearing his flannel sweatshirt; the sleeves were patched. Two men stood behind him. Imberman's spotters. The announcer stepped off the platform. With no hesitation or sign of anxiety or fright Imberman thrust his head under the bar. The spotters stood like sentries behind the enormous plates. Imberman lowered his body slowly. I heard the metal plates rattle and spin, and I clutched my Holy Name medal and prayed for him. Imberman sat with the barbell on his back; his face seemed crumpled and bewildered in the semi-darkness. He tried to stand. His knees began to buckle, and the spotters immediately gripped the barbell. It was too heavy for them, and it dropped onto the platform with a shattering sound. The weightlifters cheered and booed, and stamped their feet. I tried to reach the platform, but the aisle was blocked. I kept climbing over seats. The plates on both sides of the barbell were still rattling. Imberman was gone.

I went to every Y in the Bronx. I even took off a day from school. But no one knew anything about him. I met Harvey Rosen at the Loew's Paradise, and he told me that Imberman was peddling dope. Of course I didn't believe him. Billy told me that he saw Imberman riding in a sports car with two heavily painted Negro women. Once I even thought I saw him at the Junior Olympics on Randall's Island.

Billy never went to Notre Dame. He failed algebra and didn't even finish high school. I went to Fordham and stopped working out. I dreamed about Imberman from time to time. In my dreams he always appeared at a moment of crisis and managed to save me from all sorts of disasters. Sometimes he wore a cloak like Captain Marvel, and at other times he wore a sweatshirt with a capital "I" emblazoned on his chest. Once vultures were preparing to eat me alive, and Imberman emerged from the ground, scattered the vultures and even broke a few of their necks. Three or four times I was pursued by elephants with enormous tusks. I ran through forests and hid in caves, but the elephants caught me every time. They shrieked and charged toward me, their tusks aimed at my heart. And then, when the elephants were almost upon me, Imberman, wearing his Captain Marvel cloak, broke through the sky. He always waited until the final minute. And in no time at all he snapped off the tusks of every elephant, and slapping their enormous buttocks, he sent them packing. He never talked to me in any of the dreams. And once monkeys and ants had trapped me in a ditch, and the ants were already invading my eye sockets and armpits. I howled and waited for Imberman. I raised my ant-infested head and searched the skies and the woods for him, but Imberman never showed up. I woke with a coughing fit. Even my father was worried. I never dreamed about Imberman again.

Billy Wisnoiwiecki married the niece of a seltzer baron, and received a dowry fit for a king. The seltzer baron, a generous Armenian with a game leg, accepted Billy into the clan, and gave him a seltzer truck and the most magnificent seltzer route in the city. Billy's undisputed territory ranged from one end of Manhattan to the other. I had no such luck. I was finishing my last year at Columbia Journalism and lived in a room and a half near 116th Street. I taught English three nights a week at the George Washington adult center. I would often run into Billy and his seltzer truck on Amsterdam Avenue or Broadway, and if he happened to be going in my direction, he would drive me over. About three or four weeks ago, while I was crossing Broadway, I heard a battery of seltzer bottles booming behind me. I responded automatically. "Billy."

Dwarfed by the enormous cab of his truck, he seemed like a toy general with a seltzer bottle army. "Siggie," he said, "guess who I saw yesterday in the middle of Harlem? With a beard and a pair of cowboy boots. Your old boy friend. Bimberman."

"What?" I said.

"Sure. Even a beard couldn't hide that face. It was Bimberman."

"*I*mberman," I said, "*I*mberman."

"Imberman, Bimberman, he's still a bum. You want a ride uptown?"

"No."

Billy drove off, the bottles banging out a monotonous song. I went home. The new term was starting at the evening center and I still hadn't prepared book lists and lesson plans.

Billy was right. He did have a beard. But his pinched cheeks and enormous ears gave him away. He wore a tanker jacket with a hood. I wrote my name on the board. My fingers trembled. Imberman in my English class! The meeting seemed somehow fated. I jabbered for an hour about misplaced modifiers and Edgar Allan Poe, and then dismissed the class. Imberman left his seat, clutching his tanker jacket. His boots squeaked. I trapped him near the door.

We walked toward Broadway. Why had he joined the adult center? He didn't know any grammar, he said, and he couldn't spell. Was he looking for a clerical job? No, he wanted to be a writer. I looked at him suspiciously. Was he studying Zen? No. Had he written anything? Yes. Would he show me some of his writing? Yes. Tonight? Yes. Where? At the northeast corner of 125th Street and Lenox Avenue. Ten o'clock. See you. Goodbye.

I was there at a quarter after nine. Three pimps and a prostitute approached me, almost consecutively. The prostitute called me Daddy, and offered to take me to the Sunshine Club. She had orange hair and must have been at least sixty years old. I declined her offer, and with a ladylike smile she immediately went after someone else. The three pimps were impossible. I kept waving them off, but they still claimed me as their prize. When I refused them for the sixth or seventh time, they seemed a little offended, and walked off in different directions. I waited for the next wave of pimps, but I was left alone. At five after ten Imberman appeared. He was carrying a satchel. His beard was trimmed and his matted hair was combed. As casually as possible I asked him where he had been for the past nine years. He pointed to the satchel. Did he have time for a beer? No, sorry, he was in a hurry. He gave me the satchel, but it dropped out of my hand, and I stooped clumsily and retrieved it. When I stood up he was gone.

The manuscript was written in pencil. I sat on the cross-town bus and counted the pages. One thousand nine hundred and seventy-nine.

The entire first page of Imberman's book was illegible. I managed to decipher a word here and there in spite of Imberman's curious spelling. "Disharmoney." "Atrofie." "Greshims Lawe." I skipped fifty pages, but the writing was equally illegible. And after laboring over the manuscript I was able to make out an entire sentence. "Evry Age nedes a Robin Hoode." I tried another page. "Dont look for the Bombes to com from the Skie." I now considered myself an expert on Imberman's syntax and spelling. I skipped the next thousand pages and began reading at random. "Stay away from the Whorlots in Waco. Galveston and Taylors better. And the Beer dont make you psss so much." I read further. Imberman had the "Whorlots" pegged in half the cities of Texas, Arkansas, and Louisiana. The next fifty pages took me in and out of Mexico. And if Imberman's facts are correct, Pancho Villa is still alive, and the Mexican government can expect a revolution any day.

Somewhere around the fifteen-hundredth page I came across the following item. Imberman might have been in Georgia, or California, or New Jersey at the time. That part of the story wasn't clear. "They strapped The Boy on the back of the JunkMans Hors. They all said He tuchd LuCie Shittems tit. LuCie Shittem was 10 or 11 and The Boy was 12 maybe. They calld Him Crazy Jack." Imberman here drew a picture of the boy, and in a rather remarkable way Crazy Jack resembled Imberman himself. Hollow cheeks. Matted hair. Tremendous ears. But Imberman gave the boy a grim mouth, and an impassive stare, and it was obvious to me that the boy must have been a moron or a mute. "The JunkMan started ledeing the Hors rownd in a cirkul and Crazy Jack on the bAck of the Hors looked up at the Skie and laffd out lowd. LuCie Shittems Father took six Branches and sharpend them with A Kitchn Knife and gave one to Evrybody, even a Lady. He saw me standing outside the cirkul and wanted To give me a Branch, but I shook my head No. I watchd Crazy Jack look at the Skie all the time. An AirPlane passd and Jack moved His Arms like a SeaGull while the Hors was going rownd the cirkul. LuCie Shittems Father gave the Signul and Evrybody started whippping Jack with the Branches. LuCie Shittem huggd her Doll and laffd like a Dope evrytime the whips hit Jack. The JunkMan led the Hors rownd and rownd and the Hump on his back started to dans. One of Jacks Eyes closd and His Mouth twisted evrytime they whipppd Him, but His Arms still moved like a SeaGull. I droppd my pack. I broke open the cirkul and thruu the JunkMan on top of his Wagon and I knockd the Wagon over and a wheeel broke off and started spinnning down the Roade. I stopppd the Hors and untied Jack. LuCie

Shittem thruu her Doll at me. Her Father calld me SONOFA-
BITCH and said GO GET FINNEY. The JunkMan moand. Evrybody started moving in with the Branches and the cirkul
closed arownd me. I put Jack on my sholders and stood
infront of the Hors. FINNEY somebody said FINNEY." Here
the manuscript became illegible again. I worked for an hour
and wasn't even able to decipher another line. I thought I
saw the word "GoD."

The adult center was closed until Tuesday, and I almost
went berserk waiting for the days to pass. Sunday night,
when the waiting became unbearable, I marched down to
the ping-pong parlor on Ninety-seventh Street, challenged
one of the local champions, and lost fifteen dollars in twenty
minutes. Furious with myself, I crushed a dozen ping-pong
balls and refused to pay for them, and when the manager
threatened to call the police I ran home, locked myself in the
bathroom, and opened Imberman's satchel. I searched
through the last four hundred pages but couldn't find another word about LuCie Shittem or Crazy Jack. Tuesday
afternoon I sat in an empty theatre and watched *The Mal-
tese Falcon,* but even Sam Spade and the Fat Man couldn't
contain me, and I walked out in the middle of the show. At
the stroke of six I packed the satchel and ran downstairs. I
arrived at the adult center just before the late bell rang, and
gripping the satchel with both hands, I charged up to my
room.

Imberman's seat was empty. I retreated behind my desk
and began diagramming sentences on the board. Twice I
mistook an adverb for a pronoun, and once I put an exclama-
tion mark in the middle of a prepositional phrase. Mr.

Kriputkin, a candlemaker from Longfellow Avenue, cor-
rected me, and with one sweep of my arm I erased every
sentence from the board. The eraser shot out of my hand and
flew across the room. Mr. Kriputkin wisely covered his head.
I dismissed the class twenty minutes early, without giving
out an assignment or saying goodbye. I picked up the
satchel and left.

Yes, I went back to Lenox Avenue. I even visited the
Sunshine Club. Where's Imberman? Nobody knew. I called
up Billy Wisnoiwiecki, and twice he drove me from Dyck-
man Street down to the Bowery. I sat in the back of the
truck with the seltzer bottles and scanned every street. Billy
kept waving to me from the cab and shouting, "Bimberman,
Bimberman."

The satchel sits near my toilet seat, unclaimed. I've already deciphered over two hundred pages. The book is
packed with mysteries and paradoxes. Only Imberman can
explain them. I read a few fragments to my class at the adult
center. "A bad Dream is worse then the Fluu. You never
really recover." "The Devil is lonelie sometiMes Too." Mr.
Kriputkin was impressed. Yesterday I copied out a page
from Imberman's book and put it on the board as a grammar
exercise. "Correct the spelling first," I said, "and then take
out any word that bothers you." Most of the men and women
in the class chuckled when they saw Imberman's spelling,
and they sat with their backs hunched busily over their
desks. Only Mr. Kriputkin remained idle. "Mr. Kriputkin," I
said, "get to work." He crossed his arms. "No." he said. He
rose and stood in front of the blackboard. The class rebelled.
"Get outa the way, Kriputkin." "Dopes," Mr. Kriputkin said,

"it's poetry." He turned toward me. "Tell me, what, who is Imberman?" I told Mr. Kriputkin and the rest of the class about my first and last meeting with Imberman, and about Biceps Harvey, and the Crotona Y, and the Mr. New York City Contest. Everyone began to chatter. Mr. Kriputkin raised both hands and silenced the class. He turned toward me again. "Don't worry," he said. "You will meet with him again. Could be ten years, could be twenty. It will happen." Then he stared fiercely at the class. "Put your pencils down." He marched back to his desk. "Poetry," he said. This time no one dared to disagree.

"Farewell! . . .
Farewell! . . ."

Able!
Baker!
Charlie!
Dog!
While Ikey Bendelson and his boys were playing Hit the
Jap with a dented tin can or a cardboard jack-o'-lantern with
Tojo's face painted on it, and shouting "Gung-ho!" and all
the other phony war cries they had picked up at the RKO
Chester and the Loew's Tremont, I was learning how many
companies were in a battalion, and how many battalions
were in a division. And when Ikey would tell one of his
cousins from New Jersey how the Japs were being driven out

of caves with flame throwers, I would interrupt him to say, "They don't use flame throwers, Ikey, they use white phosphorous grenades." Of course I knew the American soldiers sometimes used flame throwers mounted on light tanks, but I still enjoyed contradicting Ikey, especially in front of his cousins. Ikey always had the same poor excuse. "Well, what do you expect, Saul's brother Leo is in the marines." And I would have to correct him again. "How many times do I have to tell you, Ikey, Leo's in the *infantry*, not the marines!"

But it wasn't Leo who taught me all about the war. It was my brother Albie. Every morning Albie would stand on his bed and mark off another day on the calendar. Then he would salute the wall and say, "Leo, I'll see you in the Solomons in two hundred and sixty-nine days." Albie was sixteen, and he kept praying that the days would merge together and make him old enough to enlist. Ordinarily it would have driven my mother out of her mind to watch the way Albie carried on, but she knew that no draft board in the world would ever accept him. I was twelve then, but I was already a full head taller than Albie. He had rickets when he was a kid, and one of his shoulders was slightly misshapen. I don't think he weighed much more than a hundred pounds. But when anyone mentioned the word "marines" Albie's gnomelike face would harden, and he looked like some fierce warrior who would have been willing to challenge a dragon or a two-ton tank. "The marines are a crock of shit. It's the 27th Infantry that's doing all the fighting in the Pacific."

Albie read every army manual he could find, and he made sure that Leo sent him all the issues of his division bulletin, *Tropic Lightning News*. Albie could have been the

official historian of Leo's regiment, because he knew everything about the 27th Infantry—its campaigns from the time
of the Spanish-American War, how many casualties it had
suffered in World War I, and why the regiment was called
the "Wolfhounds." Leo sent Albie a Japanese flag from New
Georgia and Albie draped the flag over his bed. Leo had also
confiscated an ivory-handled hari-kari knife from a dead
Japanese officer, and now the knife hung near the flag.

Albie made Leo write to us every week. And once when
Leo didn't write for three weeks and my mother was ready
to send a telegram to the War Department, Albie told her,
"Don't worry, Ma, Leo must be on some kind of secret
mission. He'll write again as soon as he can." One morning
the postman handed Albie a crumpled V-mail letter, and
he ran upstairs like a maniac and almost tore the envelope in
half, he was so eager to open it. "Albie," my mother pleaded,
"don't ruin me the letter." It turned out that Albie had been
right all the time. Leo's platoon had taken part in a secret
counter-offensive, and helped recapture an island near
Luzon. Albie socked his chest. "I knew Leo would never let
us down!" Then he took the hari-kari knife off the wall and
brandished it in front of the Japanese flag. "*Banzai*," he
shouted. "Banzai! Wait until me and Leo get together. We're
gonna drive the Nips back to Tokyo!" My mother slapped
her cheeks and motioned to me with her head. "Saul, please,
take the knife away from him." I ran around the room and
pretended that I was talking through a walkie-talkie. "Able
Company, Baker calling. How's Charlie?"

"Two idiots," my mother said, and she left. I threw Leo's
letter up in the air and then I noticed something else inside
the envelope. "Al, what's this?"

Albie put the hari-kari knife back on the wall. "Hey," he said, "it's one of those Japanese propaganda leaflets." We sat on his bed and read the leaflet together.

Farewell, American soldiers!
You are still alive? What a miracle! Do you know what awaits you in the Philippines? YOUR GRAVE! Nobody can say where it exactly is, but it is certain that it does exist somewhere in the Philippines, and you are bound to find it sooner or later, far or near. Today? Tomorrow? Who Knows?

"Holy shit," Albie said.

There are only two definite things on earth. LIFE and DEATH. The difference between LIFE and DEATH is absolute. One cannot rely upon the dead; no one can make friends with the dead; the dead can neither speak nor mingle with the living. If you insist on marching west, we (by we I mean all the living things) must bid you goodbye and stop bothering with you, because we, the living, are too busy to have anything to do with the dead.

So, officers and men, I bid you a pitiful goodbye. Today you are with the living—tomorrow, with the dead. So again, goodbye, American soldiers! . . . Farewell! . . . Farewell! . . .

Leo was a biology teacher at James Monroe High School when the war began. His job was classified as a "critical skill," and he could have stayed out of the army. But he enlisted the day after Germany declared war on the United States. Leo did not believe in violence—he had never had a fight with anyone in his life—but now he was prepared to kill every German soldier in the world. "We charge with fixed bayonets at stuffed dummies suspended from a metal rail," Leo wrote from Camp Kilmer in New Jersey, "and the sergeant yells, 'Kill, kill,' and I twist my mouth savagely and stab my dummy and watch its straw guts spill out all over the place. Give me time, I will learn to hate wholeheartedly. Ma, I wasn't born in Chelm. I know that many people on both sides will make a profit from the war, and governments will barter away lives and betray others to save themselves, but I'm still willing to fight. There are too many Hitlers in the world. Let me at least help get rid of one." When Leo finished basic training, he came home for a few days. He had never handled a rifle before. His eyes were bad because of all the days he had spent sitting hunched over his microscope, but he had still won a marksman's medal, and he let Albie wear it. Albie was fourteen at the time, and he marched up and down the block wearing Leo's medal. Ikey Bendelson hissed and called Albie a "little Hitler," and Albie chased after him with a stick, the medal clapping against his chest.

Leo took Albie and me to Bronx Park, and all the high school girls with long hair and bobby sox sang "Don't Sit Under the Apple Tree," and waved to Leo, because he was wearing a uniform. Albie walked through the park with his hands in his pockets, and kept talking to himself. "We'll fix 'em. Me and Leo. Hitler better keep ten bodyguards around him all the time." Leo bought me a big bag of peanuts and some Crackerjacks, and we feasted the elephants and the kangaroos. Albie stood near the lion pit and roared back at the lions. Leo had to drag him away. Then we went to the Sugarbowl and Leo bought me a hot fudge sundae. The fudge kept sticking to my lips and Leo called me "Little Black Sambo." Albie didn't laugh once all the time we were there. Leo touched the medal on Albie's chest. "Straighten up, soldier. Chin out. Suck in that gut." Albie's ears perked when he heard the word "soldier," and he responded instantly to Leo's commands. "You too, soldier," Leo snapped, turning to me, and I could feel my body stiffen. We marched out of the Sugarbowl, Leo keeping time. "One, two. One, two." Albie's pinched, old man's face glowed, and he reminded me of Gunga Din.

That night we helped Leo pack his duffel bag. My mother kept rocking back and forth and crying. "Leo, take care." Then she cursed Hitler, and Mussolini, and Haman—Purim was her favorite holiday!—and Tojo too. "Sarah," my father said, pointing to me, "this is the way to talk in front of Saul?" "Let him learn," my mother said bitterly, "let him learn now who are his enemies!" Leo had to leave in the middle of the night and we all waited up with him. My father wore his silk bathrobe, and with his head bent over and his paunch hanging down he looked like a comic King Solomon. "Leo," he said, "one thing, be a mensch." He tugged the tassels of his robe, and held up one hand. "Show that midget with the mustache and the rest of his gangsters, show them what David did to Goliath!" Then he broke down and started to sob. Albie walked out of the room. Leo tried to comfort my father. Albie came back with Leo's duffel bag slung over his shoulder. His face was taut and bloodless. "Leo, it's time to go." Leo picked me up and I hugged him and started to cry. "Saul, make sure you wear your galoshes when it rains." Albie took the medal off his chest. "Keep it, Al," Leo said. Albie stared at him. "But you'll get in trouble, Leo, if they catch you without your medal." "Ah," Leo said, "the sergeant says they can't afford to throw a trained soldier in the stockades. They need everybody to fight the Germans."

Then he picked up the duffel bag, leaned over and kissed my mother, my father, and me, gripped Albie's hand, and left.

Leo was never given the chance to fight the Germans. He was sent to a camp in Georgia for advanced training, and from there he was shipped off to the Pacific to join the 27th Infantry. When my mother found out, she was ready to write a letter to President Roosevelt. "Sarah," my father said, "he'll be better off. The Germans have tanks and bombs that can't be stopped." My mother calmed down.

Leo never had time to write four separate letters, so he would write one long letter that was meant for all of us. First he would write a few lines to my mother and father. "Dear Mom and Pop. They sent a Jewish chaplain over from Hawaii and he had a seder in one of the tents. My friend Augie Farinella came to the seder and ate up a whole pound of gefilte fish and finished off the wine that was supposed to have been left over for the next seder. The rabbi wanted to throw him right out of the tent. How was your seder? Does Saulie know the prayers yet? Can he ask the Four Questions?" And then he would say a few words to me. "Dear Saul. Today we have Geography Lesson Number Two. Luzon is the chief island of the Philippines, and Manila is its capital. Now you can show your teacher how smart you are. And you can tell her not to worry. One of these days we're going to throw the Japs out of Luzon. And Saul, if Mommy tells me that you know the Four Questions, I'll send you something special the next time." The rest of the letter was reserved for Albie. That was always my favorite part. Leo would tell Albie all about the flares, and the ack-ack guns, and the dumdum bullets, and the flame tanks, and sometimes he would draw little maps for Albie and show him how the machine guns were set up to hold back a Japanese attack. Once he sent home a snapshot of himself and his friend Augie. They both had ammunition belts strung crosswise over their shoulders. "Augie cracks everybody up in our squad. He keeps asking the sergeant to make him the number two gunner, but the sergeant knows what a clown he is, and he won't let him get near any of the guns."

Albie put himself in charge of answering Leo's letters. He made us write neatly and sometimes he even censored things that my mother or father wrote. "Ma, why do you gotta tell him all the time to watch out? You'll give him the creeps! Here, start another letter!" I never knew what to say to Leo, and Albie would help me out. "Tell him," he would dictate, sitting crosslegged on the floor, "tell him to send home the head of a Japanese general." Long furrows would appear on his forehead and his knees would begin to sway. "No, say: Leo, we had a block party last week, and Mr. Martinson donated twelve cases of Pepsi and everybody drank a toast to you and we made you the Mayor of the block. We all wished that you and your squad would kill at least a thousand Japs. And we also drank a toast to your friend Augie."

"But, Al," I would protest, "none of this is true. We never—"

"What's the difference? Leo'd like to hear it, wouldn't he? That's what counts. Now write it!"

About a week before Albie's seventeenth birthday a letter came from New Caledonia. Actually, it was more of a note than a letter. It didn't even have a salutation. "My friend Augie died yesterday. He was shot in the head by a sniper while we were at chow. Augie was doing an imitation of Charlie Chaplin for us. I helped him cut out a cardboard mustache, but he couldn't hold the mustache in place between his nose and his lip. The sniper shot him just as he was stooping over to pick up the mustache. We caught the sniper and we—" The rest of the letter was censored. The words were blocked out with black ink. Albie's lips twitched when he read the letter to us. My mother cried. "And here I was going to bake Haman tashen for both of them."

After that, Leo's letters were short. He hardly ever talked about the war. And then he stopped writing. "Ma," Albie said, "it's like last time, remember? Leo must be on another secret mission. He'll write soon. You'll see." And he kept lashing us. "What's the difference if Leo doesn't answer us? We still have to write him at least once a week." On the sly, my mother wrote a letter to the War Department. Albie found the letter before she had a chance to mail it, and he was furious. "You want the President to think that Leo is a sissy? He's on a secret mission!" And he tore up the letter.

The American soldiers were recapturing the Solomon Islands one after the other, and General Eisenhower was already on the way to Berlin. We had a block party almost every other week. Ikey Bendelson kept exploding stink bombs from the roofs, and he made huge cardboard effigies of Hitler and Tojo, and burned them in the street. I was going to be thirteen in a few months, and when I came home from Hebrew school, I would watch Ikey and his boys dance around the remains of Hitler's cardboard face. "Come on,"

Ikey would say to me, "spit in Hitler's eye." "I can't, Ikey, I have to study my bar mitzvah speech."

Once, in the middle of serving supper, my mother broke down. She was ladling soup, and she almost dropped the tureen. "Soon," she said, "soon they'll take Saul away from me too." Albie walked out of the room. "Sarah," my father said, "Don't be silly. The war is almost over."

The day before Germany surrendered, a letter came from Leo. It was mailed from an army hospital in New Zealand. The letter baffled us. We could hardly make out a word. "Maybe it's a joke?" my father said. "Wait for Albie. He'll read it for us." So we waited until Albie came home, and showed him the letter. "No," Albie said, "it's not a fake. It's Leo's handwriting. I can tell." And he tried to decipher the letter. His hands were shaking. "Au-gie and me . . . Give me the sta-tis-tics. How many Jews were in the Jap-an-ese ar-my? . . . Saulie, don't wor-ry a-bout me. Tell Al-bie I will . . ."

"So," my father said, "is he wounded?"

"No, I don't think so."

"What?" my mother said. "So why then is he in a hospital?"

Albie looked at the wall. "I don't know."

My mother wrung her hands. "I thought the letter would be a mitzvah, but now I see it only makes everything more of a mystery. Albie, are you sure?"

Two weeks later we received a letter from the War Department in a large brown envelope. Leo was coming home. "Sarah," my father said, and he started singing to himself, "Leo is coming home-home-home, Leo is coming home! Sarah, did you hear? His *tour of duty* is over. That's what it says in the letter. Our Leo is a hero! We'll have to have another block party. Go tell Mrs. Minowitz! I knew the other letter was a mistake. It must have been written by a maniac. Leo was wounded!"

He wasn't even wearing his uniform. He didn't limp, or have his arm in a sling. He was carrying a cloth satchel. "Look," my father said, holding one arm around me, "Saul's a man already. Two weeks and he'll be bar mitzvahed." Leo hugged and kissed my mother and father, slapped my shoulder, and then unzipped his satchel. "Here, Al." He took out a luger and three shells. The long muzzle of the luger glinted under the soft light of the living-room lamp. "Leo," I said, "I never knew that the Germans were fighting in the Pacific too. Where did you get the luger?" Leo winked mysteriously. He held out the luger to Albie. "Here." Albie put his hands in his pockets.

"Mr. Funeral Face," my father said, "so take it already."

"What am I going to do with a luger?" Albie said, and he kept his hands in his pockets. "Thanks, Leo. . . . Give it to Saul."

"Please," my mother said, "put away the gun. It could shoot off any minute. Who can trust a German gun?"

I took the luger from Leo, carried it into the bedroom, and put it in my drawer near my chemistry set and my checkerboard.

"Leo," I heard my mother say, "sit down, eat. I baked you some Haman tashen."

"Did you ever see such a woman? Purim is still nine months away and she bakes Haman tashen."

"When my Leo comes home, this to me is Purim!"

I touched the handle of the luger and listened to my mother talk about the block party.

"So we figured after we come from shul we would take the rebbe with us and go home. Who needs Gluckstern's! We'll have the party right on the block. This way I can say I invited the whole block to Saul's bar mitzvah!"

"The schnorrer," my father said. "She wants presents from everybody."

"Who needs presents! We'll have a party for Leo and for Saul, and who knows, maybe the Japs—they should only croak!—will surrender by then, and it will turn out to be a victory celebration too. Albie, where are you going? I never saw such a boy. . . . He goes downstairs without a jacket and he doesn't even say goodbye!"

That night Leo and I took a walk to Crotona Park. We sat on the rocks above Indian Lake and threw pebbles and match sticks into the water. The pebbles made ripples in the water and sank quickly, and most of the match sticks floated and were carried across the lake. The moon shone on Leo's face and made his cheeks glow, but his eyes remained in the dark.

"Leo," I said, "how many Japs did you kill?"

His cheeks kept glowing.

"How many?"

He pulled his head back and now the moon lit up one of his ears.

"I don't know, Saul. I was only an ammo bearer."

"Leo, can I keep the luger?"

"Sure."

We walked home. Leo sat on the stoop. "You go up, Saul, I'll stay down here for a little while and smoke a cigarette."

I went upstairs. I walked into the bedroom and saw Albie

sitting on the floor. My drawer was open. He held the luger
in his left hand and aimed it at the ceiling. Then he placed
the muzzle against his forehead and pulled the trigger twice.

"Albie!"

He put the luger away and closed the drawer.

"You shouldn't play with a gun like that. It could be
loaded."

"Don't worry about me. I know how to handle guns. You
can keep your lousy luger!"

"Hey, Al, you think Leo took the luger from a German
spy?"

Albie took the pillow and the blanket from his bed.

"What are you doing?"

"I'm moving into the living room. I don't want to sleep in
the same room with Leo and you."

"What's the matter with you, Al? Are you a nut?"

"Leo's the *nut*, not me!" Albie turned his head away and
held his hand over his eyes. I watched his jaw move up and
down. He was crying. "Why'd he have to crack up for? Is
that how he's going to get even for Augie and all the other
guys of the 27th who were killed in the Solomons and the
Philippines? I thought we were going to fight the Japs
together. He should have died better than come home like
this!"

I swung him around and grabbed his wrists. "Take that
back!" My mother came into the room. "What's the commotion? Albie, why is your pillow on the floor?"

Albie picked up the pillow. I didn't feel like fighting with
him any more.

We drove home from the synagogue in my father's
battered 1937 Nash. Albie was still wearing his yamulka,

and it kept falling off his head every time the car swerved. It was the smallest yamulka my father could find, but it was still a size too big for Albie, and it hid almost half of his head. Everybody was talking about the way I had read the Haftarah. Leo was driving the car.

"A regular Leibele Waldman," the rabbi said. He was sitting between my mother and father. Some crumbs from my mother's sponge cake were caught in his beard. "Mazel tov! Saul, one day you'll be a cantor."

"Rabbi," my mother said, "to you goes all the credit. After all, who taught him how to read the Haftarah?"

My father poked the rabbi with his thumb. He had already drunk three glasses of wine. "Rabbi, it's right you should be riding in a car on Shabbas? If the shammas finds out, he'll throw you out from shul!"

My mother stared blackly at my father. Her look silenced him. "My comedian over there!"

The rabbi smiled behind his beard. "For Saul's bar mitzvah party I will ride in a car!" His beard moved unevenly as he spoke, and a crumb fell in his lap.

There was a barrier in front of the block, and when our car arrived the barrier was removed for us, and we drove up to the wooden platform that had been built for the block party in the middle of the street. Star-spangled bunting was strung across the fire escapes on both sides of the street. A female accordionist with a double chin sat on the platform. I read the paper signs attached to the banners. "Buy at Moisha's." "Drop Dead, Adolf." "Welcome Home, Leo." Ikey Bendelson's cardboard effigies hung from every lamppost on the block. Tojo's evil face was chalked all over the sidewalks. He was drawn with a mustache, without a mus-

tache, with a broken neck, with an obscene smile, with
donkey's ears, without a nose, and once or twice he appeared
as a beetle or a roach with unmistakable slanted eyes.
Behind the platform stood a long table stacked with pastrami sandwiches, sour pickles, and bottles of Pepsi-Cola.
People swarmed around the table and sometimes bottles
overturned and sandwiches dropped and were immediately
squashed. Ackerman the druggist, holding a pastrami sandwich in one hand and a megaphone in the other, stood on
the top step of the platform. Ikey Bendelson, wearing a
dented air-raid warden's helmet, stood behind him. The chin
strap of the helmet was broken and banged against his belt.
"Attention!" Ackerman shouted into the megaphone, and we
all sang "God Bless America." Two men had to help the accordionist stand up. Her skirt kept billowing and her garters
showed. She was having a wonderful time. "Where's the bar
mitzvah boy?" Ackerman said, winking at me, and I walked
up the steps of the platform. Everybody clapped. My mother
and father stood near the platform, holding hands. Albie
stood under a lamppost and tried to keep the sun out of his
eyes. Hitler swung over his head. The cardboard legs of the
effigy almost touched the top of his yamulka. Leo took out a
handkerchief and wiped his forehead. Ackerman handed me
the megaphone. I thanked my mother and father, Ackerman,
and everybody on the block for making the party, and then I
prayed that all our soldiers would be safe, that the war
would end, and that there would never be another war
again. "Today our Saul is a man," Ackerman said. "Three
cheers for the bar mitzvah boy!" The accordionist played
Shain Vi Di Levone. Ackerman stood in front of the
accordionist and clapped his hands. Husbands and wives,

sisters and brothers, girlfriends and boyfriends started pairing off. The rabbi danced with the local beauty, a sixteen-year-old-girl with tremendous breasts. Ikey Bendelson made a machine gun with his fingers and went around shooting everybody. "Ra-ta-ta-ta-ta!" Albie stayed under the lamppost. He didn't even protest when Ikey Bendelson called Leo a marine. Leo kept wiping his forehead with the handkerchief. "Ra-ta-ta-ta-ta! Charge the marine!" Ackerman raised one arm and the accordionist stopped playing. "Ladies and gentlemen, now it is my pleasure to introduce to you a true lion of Judah—a young man who single-handedly killed over two hundred Japs, and wounded God knows how many more! Here he is, the pride of the marines, our own Leo Simonson. Come up here, Leo, we love you!" Leo wouldn't put away his handkerchief and my mother had to push him up the steps of the platform. Albie put his hands in his pockets and walked toward the end of the block. The sun was beginning to set and the effigies hanging from the lampposts now formed grotesque shadows in the street. Ikey Bendelson danced around the platform. "Ra-ta-ta-ta! Kill the marine!"

Mr. Martinson, the grocer, cupped his hands over his mouth and shouted, "Tell us, Leo, tell us how you smashed the Nips!"

Albie sat down near the empty lot at the end of the block.

"Ra-ta-ta-ta-ta!"

My mother looked at Leo and her chin dropped. "Leo, what's wrong? Somebody give him a glass of Pepsi!"

The men and women standing near the platform clapped their hands and stamped their feet. "Leo! Leo! Leo!"

The star-spangled banners streamed overhead.

Ackerman blew into the megaphone and handed it to Leo. Leo's lips worked and he started to say something, but the megaphone dropped and he put his hands over his ears. Then he hurried down the steps of the platform and left the block party.

Ackerman picked up the megaphone, paused, and said, "Three cheers . . . three cheers for Leo and all the Simonsons!"

I glanced at the empty lot, but Albie was gone.

The accordionist started playing "When the Lights Go On Again," and Mr. Martinson linked my mother's arm in his, and sang along with the music.

"Martinson," my mother said, "let me go, please. I have to find my Leo."

"Sarah," my father said, "how can you leave the party? It would be a scandal! Leo's all right. He went upstairs."

Mrs. Martinson wanted to give me a bar mitzvah kiss, but I ducked under her chin and ran toward the sidewalk. Tojo's face was everywhere. Tojo with a patch over one eye, Tojo with an arrow through his head, Tojo wearing a cape. I ran faster and the faces on the sidewalk became indistinct. And now I could only recognize a random nose or an occasional slanted eye. When I reached our house I rested for a minute on the stoop. "Ra-ta-ta-ta-ta!" I turned around and saw Ikey Bendelson behind me. He was holding his helmet and standing on one of Tojo's faces. With his free hand he drew up the corner of his left eye. "Kill," he said, "kill the marine!" I ran upstairs.

"Leo, I don't care if you never killed a Jap. You don't have to be a hero. I wouldn't even care if you were a spy! You're still my brother."

He was sitting on Albie's bed and smoking a cigarette. His

hand was shaking and the smoke from the cigarette curled toward the ceiling erratically. Drops of perspiration kept falling from his ear and his chin. The window behind him was open and I could hear the accordionist playing "Anchors Aweigh." He smiled and gave me his handkerchief. "Here, Saul. You shouldn't be crying on your bar mitzvah day."

"You don't have to explain anything to me, Leo. I don't care!"

"Listen, Saul, listen to me. It was Augie who kept me going. I think he was even more scared than I was. Everybody was scared, except maybe a few screwballs. But Augie always managed to shut out the war for me and the other guys in the squad. He never let anything get too serious. Even while we were in combat Augie would jump around and pretend that somebody put a bullet up his ass. The sergeant kept shouting at him and threatened to leave him in the jungle, but he knew we couldn't get along without Augie's antics." Leo closed his eyes, raised his chin, and let the smoke blow out of his nose. "Saul, he was the ugliest guy in the world. He had a nose that would have put Pinocchio's to shame!"—I laughed and wiped my eyes with Leo's handkerchief—"And everywhere you looked on his face there was a pock mark, a pimple, or a hole. How they ever let that guy in the army I'll never know. He couldn't pick up a shovel, or open a can, and if not for me he would have slept without a tent over his head. Saul, he was completely helpless. Maybe if he hadn't clowned around all the time, he would have driven us all insane." I couldn't tell if Leo was laughing or crying, so I gave him back his handkerchief. "You know, Saul, if I had met Augie while I was in basic training, I would have called him a schmo and stayed away from him. I had a war to fight and I didn't want to be around any goof-offs. I used to sit on my bunk while the other guys were shooting crap or playing stud, and see myself capturing Germans and saving Jews. And then later when I saw heads crack open and arms and legs swell up and turn green, and when I saw tanks ride over dead bodies, I didn't want to save anybody. I just wanted to stay alive. But with Augie around things were still all right. He ignored the Japs completely. He had his own private war with all the scorpions and centipedes in the Pacific. Whenever he saw a scorpion he'd howl and go running for his bayonet. That's the only time he ever used his bayonet. To chase after scorpions. He'd challenge the scorpion to a duel, and all the guys in the squad would take sides and boo either Augie or the scorpion. Sometimes he'd chase the scorpion into the jungle, or if the scorpion decided to come after him, he would back down and hide behind the sergeant or me."

Leo lit another cigarette. His hand was still shaking, and he almost dropped the match. He offered me a cigarette.

"Sure," I said uneasily. "I can smoke. I'm thirteen."

The cigarette tasted bitter, and I kept coughing smoke in Leo's face. Leo drove the smoke away with his hand. I heard Ikey Bendelson fire his machine gun.

"You know, Saul, when that sniper killed Augie, I think I went out of my mind a little. All of us did. We burned the Jap out of his tree with a flame thrower. His body was all charred and kept sizzling, and we all took turns and pissed on him. And for the next two or three days I went around like a wildman and mutilated the body of every dead Jap I could find. And at night I would sit in my foxhole with my helmet over my face and cry. I was afraid, Saul, I was afraid. Every time we'd go out on a patrol, I kept dropping cartridges all over the place. The sergeant said if I kept it up I'd lead the Japs right back to our bivouac. If a tree would shake, I'd run for cover right away. And when the flares went up before an attack, I'd hide in my foxhole and cover my head with a poncho. They switched me over to another squad, but it didn't help. Then they sent me behind the lines to this two-room hospital that was set up near the mouth of a cave. I played ping-pong with a few of the orderlies, but most of the time I unpacked medical supplies and helped the stretcher bearers carry the wounded into the cave whenever the Japs decided to bomb us. I thought they were going to let me stay at the hospital and help out, but they sent me back to my old squad after a week. I didn't panic or anything; I just sat in my foxhole all day and invented little games. I'd write out the names of every player in the American League that I could remember, and then I'd assemble eight teams and make out a schedule. I'd play off the games using a deck of cards. Both black aces would be a homer, the king of spades would be a triple, each queen would be a double, you know. Then I'd flip the deck and play. Joe DiMaggio. Deuce of diamonds. Strike out! I let DiMaggio and Hank Greenberg play on the same team. And every time Greenberg came up to bat, I'd cheat a little, and pull out a black ace or a king. After fifty games he hit seventy-eight home runs. I played over five hundred games in less than two weeks. And then at night I'd think about Augie. And sometimes I would pretend he was sitting next to me in the foxhole and we'd talk or play checkers. I forgot about the flares, and the bombs, and the snipers in the trees.

The mortar shells would burst over my head and I kept talking to Augie or playing my baseball games. And then they sent me to New Zealand."

Leo nibbled the end of his cigarette and the tobacco began to shred. I sat down next to him on the bed. "Everything will be all right, Leo. The hell with the Japs and the war!"

"You know, Saul, I think I'm going to enlist again."

I swallowed some smoke and my eyes began to tear and I almost choked. Leo put out his cigarette and patted my back.

Somebody knocked on the front door. Ikey's father was standing in the hall. He was holding Albie by the collar of his shirt. Albie's yamulka was pulled down over his left eye. Leo came over, and Mr. Bendelson released Albie. "I'm sorry, Leo," he said, "but he was throwing stones at my kid. I didn't want to bother your mother, so I figured I'd bring him up to you. What's wrong with him? He was crying and cursing and he almost took out Ikey's eye with a stone. What did Ikey ever do to him?" Mr. Bendelson shook my hand. A Pepsi-Cola bottle stuck out of his jacket pocket. "Congratulations, Saul." Then he shook Leo's hand and left.

Albie walked past us and went into the bedroom. Leo took out another cigarette. His hand kept shaking, and I had to light the cigarette for him. I blew out the match, crumpled it, and put it in my pocket. Leo walked into the bedroom. I followed him. Albie was sitting on his bed. He wasn't wearing his yamulka any more, and he was holding something in his hand. It was Leo's marksman's medal.

"Al," Leo said, "let's go over to the recruiting station tomorrow and enlist together, huh?" He was smiling.

Albie raised his deformed shoulder and stood up. "Here," he said, his mouth working venomously, "I don't want your lousy medal!"

He walked out of the bedroom. Leo put the medal on the dresser. A strand of loose hair touched the bridge of his nose and divided his forehead in half.

"Leo," I said, "you'll see. Everything will be all right."

I spent the next morning taking inventory of all my bar mitzvah presents. I had three Parker pens, two twenty-five-dollar War Bonds, a leather-covered copy of *The Wisdom of Maimonides*, a gold-dipped draidl, a hand-carved mezuzah from Palestine, a prayer shawl embroidered with silver thread, a pearl-handled hunting knife (from Albie), a catcher's mitt, a chess set with imitation ivory pieces, a pictorial history of Purim with hand-painted illuminations on every second page (from my mother), Mark Twain's *Life on the Mississippi* and a fifty-dollar War Bond (from Leo), seventeen ten-dollar bills, and five five-dollar bills.

I gave Leo one of my Parker pens. "See if it writes, Leo." I found a bottle of Waterman's blue-black ink. The pen sucked up the ink in the bottle as if it were trying to breathe. Leo wrote his name, my name, and Albie's name on a sheet of loose-leaf paper.

"Leo," my mother kept saying, "you sure you're all right?" She kneaded her hand over her heart. "You gave me such a scare! I thought I would croak in the street. Leo, take some more cake. I baked it special for Saul's bar mitzvah."

Leo asked my father if he could borrow the car. He wanted to take a ride to Orchard Beach. "Sure," my father said, "but why Orchard Beach? It's not open yet. Go better to City Island. You'll find some nice merchandise over there." My father winked mischievously and rolled his eyes. I would have gone with Leo, but I wanted to finish my inventory. He said goodbye to all of us. Albie didn't answer him.

The handle of Albie's hunting knife felt smooth and cold. I put the knife on Albie's side of the dresser. "I don't want any presents from you. And I have an extra Parker pen, but I'm going to give it to Ikey."

My father took his balalaika and a beach chair and went with my mother to Crotona Park. Albie sat on his bed, and I sat on mine. I looked over my presents again, and I tried to figure out how much my War Bonds would be worth in twenty-five years. I heard Ikey Bendelson playing Hit the Jap in the street. I was tired of sitting on my bed, and I wanted to go downstairs and show Ikey Leo's luger and some of my presents. I walked over to the dresser and opened the drawer.

"Okay, wise guy," I said, "where'd you put it?"

Albie didn't answer me.

"Where'd you put my luger?"

I leaned over and shook Albie's shoulders. I could feel his body rattle. "Answer me, Al, or I'll shake the life out of you."

"I didn't take your luger."

I ran into the living room and unzippered Leo's satchel. I turned the satchel over and shook it, but no shells came out. I sat on the floor and probed inside the satchel with my hand. Albie was standing over me. The pouches under his eyes turned black. I threw the satchel across the room and ran toward the front door. I heard Albie moan. I ran down the steps two at a time and almost tumbled into the police-man. His nose jutted out crookedly and his chin was covered with stubble, but he smiled kindly. He knew that I was Leo's brother. Leo had been found in an empty lot near Orchard Beach. All he had in his pockets was a wallet and my Parker pen.

The doctor had given my mother a sedative, but even in her sleep she called, "Leo, Leo." My father walked like a spook from room to room. He had turned his new silk robe into a mourner's costume, rending it with a razor. One of his half-detached sleeves kept flapping against his side. Albie sat on the bedroom floor. He wore his yamulka and held Leo's medal against his chest. He rocked back and forth on his knees, but the yamulka did not fall off. His eyes were vacant and his back was bent. His whole body seemed misshapen. My mother woke up in the middle of the night and came into the bedroom. She looked at Albie's twisted face, and for a moment she forgot her own sorrow. She leaned over and kissed him. "Albie," she said, "eat something. You'll die." Albie's eyes were still vacant.

Race Day at Hiawatha

ARE COMING BACK FROM THE WAR IN EUROPE AND MUST TRAVEL
FROM PLACE TO PLACE BY TRAIN. SO THERE ISN'T ENOUGH ROOM
FOR OTHER PEOPLE. THAT'S WHY WE WON'T BE ABLE TO COME UP
FOR THE RACE TOMORROW. OF COURSE WE'LL STILL BE CHEERING
FOR THE GOLDEN HAWK.

OUR BOYS ARE BRINGING THE JAPS TO THEIR KNEES AND THERE'S
TALK GOING AROUND THAT WE'VE DEVELOPED SOME SECRET WEAPON
THAT WILL BE ABLE TO WIPE OUT A THOUSAND JAPS AT A TIME.
IT LOOKS LIKE UNCLE EDDIE WON'T HAVE TIME TO FORM THE
MACCABEE BRIGADE.

WE RECEIVED YOUR CAMP REPORT CARD. I'M GLAD TO HEAR THAT

161

YOU ARE DOING SO WELL IN GAMES AND SPORTS. TRY TO BE A LITTLE
MORE POLITE. AND MAKE SURE YOU WASH EVERY DAY.
REMEMBER ME TO UNCLE ED AND BE SURE TO OBEY ALL

And that's when Ascher swiped the letter. I tried to make
him give it back, but he pinned my arms with his knees and
put his hand over my mouth. "Dopey," he said, "you want
Uncle Eddie to find out?" So we crawled out of the bunkhouse. Sig wanted to come with us, but Ascher said no. Only
the Captain and his Aide are supposed to go out on a
scouting mission. Ascher gave me a cockamanie, and I licked
it in the dark and put it on. "Hirohito?" I said.

"No. Tojo."

Ascher has cockamanies all over his body. Hirohitos,
Tojos, and Hitlers. But Hitler is a little out of style now, and
Ascher only has one or two on his left leg. Ascher never goes
swimming because of the cockamanies. Hirohito, Tojo, and
Hitler cockamanies are illegal at Hiawatha. Also cockamanies that show naked girls. But Ascher doesn't have any
of those. At the beginning of the summer the Destroyer
caught Sig with a Tojo cockamanie, and he ducked him in
Lake Hiawatha. The Destroyer can tear telephone books
and lift the Golden Hawk over his head with one hand.
Now you know why Ascher has to be careful with the
cockamanies. He wears his Gangbusters sweatshirt all the
time, and he never undresses when the Destroyer is around.
The Destroyer was playing poker in the latrine with the
other counselors, and Ascher knew he wouldn't be back
before ten, so that's why we didn't have to hurry. Uncle
Eddie was standing under the floodlight outside Hiawatha
House, and was knocking a nail into the bulletin board. He

was wearing khaki shorts and a Hiawatha polo shirt. "What a target," Ascher said, staring at Uncle Eddie's elephant-sized ass. Then he sat down on his knees, held out his arms, and made believe that he was a bazooka. "Come on, Dopey, fire me!" So I stood behind him, aimed his arms, and said, "Fire one!" And after we bombarded the bulletin board, the floodlight, Uncle Eddie's ass, and every window in Hiawatha House, Ascher stood up and said, "Come on." We crawled under the wire fence behind the bunkhouses, and now we were on Maccabee land. Uncle Eddie is in charge of the Maccabees too, but most of the time he's at Hiawatha. The Destroyer says that Maccabee is a "charity" camp, and maybe that's why they always win the trophy. All the Maccabees come from Brownsville, and Torpedo Tepelwitz's father is a gangster. We stayed away from the dirt road, because if any of the Maccabee counselors caught us and brought us back to Hiawatha we would both be locked up for sure in Uncle Eddie's Dungeon. Ascher is the only one in our bunkhouse who's ever been inside the Dungeon, and he says that it's the worst place in the world. Bats with crooked wings fly all around, and beetles, bugs, and termites crawl on the rafters and on every wall. Ascher had the shakes for a week after Uncle Eddie let him out of the Dungeon. So we were extra careful. When we came to Maccabee House, Ascher gave the signal, and I took off my shoes. "The Maccabees are a bunch of dopes," Ascher said. "They didn't even leave any sentries outside." He took out his pocket Eveready.

"Ascher, what if the Maccabees see the beam?"

Ascher gave me one of his why-are-you-such-a-jerk? looks. Then he held his hand over the bulb and focused the Eveready until the beam was the size of a grapfruit pit.

Leave it to Ascher! He put me in charge of his shoes, and after opening the screen door, we went looking for the Maccabees' trophy room.

Ascher found the trophy first. It was sitting on a broken phonograph box outside the counselors' latrine. "Call this a trophy room?" Ascher examined the trophy, and then let me look at it. Uncle Eddie started the Canoe Races in 1928, and the Maccabees have trimmed the Hiawathans now seventeen years in a row. Last year Ascher was our helmsman and we almost won the race, but Torpedo Tepelwitz rammed his paddle into our canoe, and Ascher fell overboard. Ascher didn't talk to anyone for the rest of the summer, and he spent the winter making plans for this year's race.

"Come on, Dopey, let's take the trophy. It belongs to us anyway. I'll fix Torpedo this year."

"You promised, Ascher. No stealing. Uncle Eddie'll disqualify us."

"Stop whining. Honestly, Dopey, I don't know why I ever made you my Aide in the first place. All right, we won't steal it. We'll take it in the shithouse and put it on one of the toilet seats. Okay?"

We heard a noise inside the counselors' latrine. Somebody whistled, and seven Maccabees, armed with hammers and hunting knives, surrounded us. Torpedo Tepelwitz was with them. Torpedo only has one good eye. A gang of colored kids caught him on an empty lot in Flatbush and burned out his left eye, and now Torpedo always wears a patch over the burned-out eye. And if he wants to give anybody the treatment, he takes off the patch and makes you look at the eye. Torpedo ran away from home when he was ten because his brother, Tojo Tepelwitz, told him that the Japs were taking over California and New Mexico and were torturing all the

Jews. Torpedo went as far as Kansas City before he was picked up. He was carrying a whole arsenal: two zip guns, a kerosene bomb, a spike, and an ice pick. Ascher's the only camper at Hiawatha who isn't afraid to stand up to Torpedo. That's why Ascher has such a reputation.

"Hey, men," Torpedo said, "look who's here. The great Ascher and his chief stooge, Dopey Diddleman."

One of the Maccabees jabbed my ass with the point of his hunting knife. I moved closer to Ascher. Torpedo grabbed Ascher's ear and mine and knocked our heads together.

"Torpedo, give 'em both another earthquake."

Torpedo knocked our heads together again.

"Earthquakes, earthquakes," all the Maccabees shouted, and Torpedo kept knocking our heads together. Ascher dropped the trophy. I started to cry.

"Okay, Ascher boy," Torpedo said, "go down on your ass now and kiss the trophy."

Ascher refused and Torpedo slapped him twice. I saw the red marks on Ascher's cheeks. Torpedo borrowed a hunting knife from one of the Maccabees. He put the blade near Ascher's eye. "How would you like people to call you One-Eyed Ackerman, huh?"

All the Maccabees cheered.

"Kiss the trophy, Ascher. Now."

Ascher dropped down and kissed the trophy. The Maccabees danced around him, singing Indian war songs, and then ran outside. Torpedo stole our shoes. Ascher was still on his knees. His back was hunched over and it kept shaking. "Ascher," I said. He was crying. He threw up near the trophy.

"Come on, Ascher, before the counselors come."

I grabbed his arm and pulled him toward the door. He looked a little dazed. I pushed him out the door, and he started running barefoot toward the lake. He was better now. I hopped after him.

"Ascher," I said, "you forgot your Eveready."

He didn't answer me.

The Pride of Judah was lying on its side near the lake. Our canoe, the Golden Hawk, was still inside Hiawatha House. The Pride of Judah has slat seats and everything, and its gunwales are covered with metal, and it's almost twice as heavy as the Golden Hawk. Ascher stripped our whole canoe, and now we have to kneel on the floorboards when we paddle. But Ascher says we have to suffer a little if we want to win the race. And when the Captain says something we listen.

I stood near the Pride of Judah and tried to think of all the hexes I knew. Ascher took out his pocket corkscrew and started drilling the bottom of the canoe. After he drilled through the canvas covering, I tried to stop him. He pushed me away. I jumped up and down near the canoe. "Ascher, we'll be disqualified for sure. Is that how you want to win the race?"

"Don't worry, Dopey, I'm not going to drill all the way through. The pressure from the water will do half the work. The canoe won't start leaking until the middle of the race." He sat on the Pride of Judah and started drilling in another place. "They won't blame us. Nobody will know what happened. When Ascher Ackerman does something, it has to work out."

Ascher's face twisted every time the corkscrew turned. And the way he looked, I was a little afraid of him.

"Ascher, I want to get even with Torpedo too. But not like this."

"Shut up," he said, and kept turning the corkscrew. Then he called me over, and I had to help him plug up the holes with mud. "See," he said, "now nobody will know the difference."

We walked back to Hiawatha territory. The Destroyer was waiting for us inside our bunkhouse. All the other campers were lined up near the wall. The Destroyer took Ascher and me and threw us against the wall. "All right, Ascher, what were you and Dopey doing outside after curfew?"

The other campers bent their heads. Ascher hissed.

"Answer me," the Destroyer said, "before I throw all of you inside the Dungeon." Sig started to shake. Little Wally Morgenthau peed in his pants.

I volunteered. "We had to take a leak, and you were playing cards inside the latrine, so we walked down to the lake. And while we were down there we started figuring out tactics for tomorrow."

The Destroyer was still suspicious, but he sent us back to our bunks. Ascher stood near the wall. "Come on," I said.

"No," Ascher said, "I'm not moving until he apologizes."

The Destroyer threw Ascher on top of his bunk. "Wait until after the race." The Destroyer left. We sat on our bunks and watched Ascher. He signaled to Sig. Sig reached under his mattress and pulled out a cigarette. His hands were shaking. He lit the cigarette for Ascher and then gave it to him.

"What if the Destroyer comes back?" Little Wally Morgenthau said, his pants already stinking from pee. "The Destroyer," he said again. We all silenced him. Ascher sat and smoked in the dark. Sig had one of his coughing fits.

He's allergic to smoke. But smoke or no smoke, he always stays near the Chief.

"Chief," Sig said, after the coughing fit, "are we gonna win tomorrow?"

Ascher smoked his cigarette. Then he said, "Come on, hit the sack. On the double." We unfolded our blankets and obeyed the Chief. Little Wally Morgenthau apologized to every camper in the bunkhouse. We all forgave him, because he's only seven. I stayed up all night and thought about the race. Torpedo and the Maccabees deserve whatever they get. This is war! Ascher cried out once in the middle of the night: "Gimme back my eye!" No one else heard him. I ran over to his bunk. "Ascher, you okay?" He was sleeping. His face was covered with sweat.

"Okay, Torpedo," I said, "everything goes."

The Destroyer is the official bugler for both camps. And every morning at six on the dot, Saturdays and Sundays included, he gives three blasts on his bugle and everyone in Sullivan County wakes up. It's impossible to sleep through one of the Destroyer's bugle calls. In fact, the Destroyer's bugle is the only thing in the world that can wake Ascher up. At five-thirty I woke every camper except Ascher and we went down to the latrine with our towels and a roll of toilet paper. We sang the Hiawatha pep song, and with Ascher still asleep I became the Acting Chief, and I went around slapping everybody's ass and telling them to shape up. We had an inspection in the latrine and I gave Sig three hundred demerits because he let his towel fall inside one of the johns. We sat on the johns and waited for the Destroyer's bugle. At six o'clock the ceiling and the walls of the latrine started to shake. Sig cursed the Destroyer and his bugle, and Torpedo Tepelwitz too. Then he gave out cockamanies to everybody. I put a Hirohito near my left armpit and a Tojo under my belly button. We compared cockamanies and started singing dirty songs. Ascher came inside the latrine. We shut up quick and stood at attention near the johns. Sig saluted the Chief. Ascher called me over and we had a conference near the piss trough. Little Wally Morgenthau waddled across the latrine, holding his ass, and pretended to be Uncle Eddie. "Boys," he said, "let's have a good, clean race." We waited for the Chief to laugh. Ascher gave Wally twenty-five demerits and made him stand inside the shower stall. "Oh, oh," Sig said to me, "we better watch out. The Chief has it in for all of us." We heard Little Wally crying inside the shower stall. "Remember," Ascher said, "low, low. When we're inside the canoe, keep your ass on the ground. All the time. And if Torpedo tries to ram us, I'll fix him this time." He crouched down. "Low, low."

We all crouched near the Chief.

"Low, low," little Wally Morgenthau said, and the Chief let him out of the shower and canceled his demerits. But Ascher wouldn't smile or anything. That's the way he was last year before the race. This year he's even worse!

We went back to the bunkhouse. The Destroyer inspected our bunks. "Shape up," he said. "You want your Moms and Dads to think you're all a bunch of slouches?" The Destroyer made Ascher tuck in his blanket. Then we followed him down to Hiawatha House. We filed into the mess hall two at a time. Most of the parents who came for the race were sitting at a long table near the door. I recognized Ascher's father right away. He owns a thousand barges, and he sends them up and down every river in America. Ascher wants to be the captain of one of his father's barges, and he's going to let all of us be his crew. I'm going to be Ascher's pilot, of course. Little Wally Morgenthau's father came over to our table. He shook everybody's hand. He gave the Destroyer an envelope, and thanked him for taking care of Wally. The Destroyer patted Wally's can. Uncle Eddie put on a skull-cap and said grace. He bowed his head and thanked God that we had enough food, and that the war would soon be over. After breakfast all the kids met with their parents. Uncle Eddie kept putting his arms around the kids and talked to every parent. He was still wearing his skullcap.

At ten-thirty Uncle Eddie blew his whistle, and Ascher, me, and Sig went inside Hiawatha House and carried out the Golden Hawk. All the Hiawathans cheered. Little Wally Morgenthau carried the paddles. We brought the Golden Hawk down to the lake. The Maccabees were already waiting near the Pride of Judah. Torpedo Tepelwitz was wearing Ascher's shoes. He touched the patch over his left eye. All the parents from both camps crowded around the lake. The counselors stood behind the canoes and made bets on the sly and I heard Denny Lipshitz, the head counselor of the Maccabees, give the Destroyer ten-to-one odds that Torpedo's crew would take the Golden Hawk by at least ten strokes. The Destroyer chickened out. Denny kept taunting him. "I thought Ascher Ackerman was a pro." He could see that the Destroyer wasn't going to bet, so he said, "Don't worry, we'll torpedo your canoe like last year." All the Maccabee counselors laughed. Uncle Eddie tuned up his megaphone. "Mothers and Fathers," he said, "and Campers of all ages, today you will witness the Eighteenth

Annual Hiawatha-Maccabee Championship Canoe Race. Rowing for Camp Maccabee will be Barney Krinchuk, Slats Shapiro, and Howie 'Torpedo' Tepelwitz." Somebody lit a firecracker. Uncle Eddie scowled for a second. "*And,*" Uncle Eddie said, smiling again. Everybody could tell that he was rooting for us. "Rowing for Camp Hiawatha will be Sig Klein, Davey Diddleman, and Ascher Ackerman. With Ascher at the helm." All the Hiawathans bunched together near our canoe and shouted, "Two, four, six, eight, who do we appreciate? Ascher, Ascher, 'ray!" Little Wally held up the paddles. Torpedo held his nose. Uncle Eddie quieted the Hiawathans. "Boys," he said, "remember, you're rowing for your camps. "Let's have a good, clean race." He signaled to Denny Lipshitz and the Destroyer with his megaphone, and the two head counselors launched the Judah and the Hawk. Little Wally Morgenthau gave us our paddles. "I hope their canoe sinks," he said, and I flipped him once on the ear. "What's that for?" Wally said, holding his ear. The Destroyer tuned up his bugle. "Okay, men," Uncle Eddie said, "man the boats." The Destroyer raised his bugle and gave three blasts. I almost tripped. Sig dropped his paddle. "Come on," Ascher said, and he pushed us both toward the canoe. We heard the Maccabees sound their war cry. Torpedo and his boys were already inside the Pride of Judah. We caught up to the Golden Hawk, gripped the gunwales, and jumped in. The Destroyer kept blowing the bugle, and my ears started to ring. Ascher said something to me. I couldn't hear him. He hit me with the end of his paddle, and I almost fell overboard. "Low," he said, "low." I crouched down and rested my knees on the floor of the canoe. The Pride of Judah was already twenty strokes ahead of us. "Low," Ascher said, and we started to paddle. Ascher cursed me and Sig and steered the canoe. "Why wouldn't they hold the race on the Neversink, why? There's no current here or anything. Any dope can handle a canoe in dead water." I wanted to tell the Chief to shut up and steer, but he would have thrown the bailing pot at me or hit me over the head with his paddle. So I kept quiet and rowed.

Torpedo stood up for a second near the bow of the Judah and taunted us. "What's the matter, Ascher boy, can't you and your fairies row fast enough?" Then he sat down and ordered his boys, "Row, row!" I prayed that the Judah would sink on the spot, but nothing happened. Maybe the mud that me and Ascher used to plug the holes dried up and made the Judah watertight. Torpedo reached the other side of the lake. I could hear all the Maccabees cheer. Me and Sig were going like maniacs. Our paddles chopped the surface of the lake and kept splashing water inside the Hawk. Ascher went to work with his bailing pot. The canoe began to spin for a second, and Ascher dropped the pot and grabbed his paddle. Over Ascher's shoulder I watched Torpedo stand on the bank of the lake and wiggle his ass for a second. Then he launched the Judah. "We'll never catch up," Sig said. Ascher poked him in the ribs with his paddle. "Shut up." The Judah came toward us. Our bows almost touched. Torpedo taunted us again. He dangled Ascher's shoe in his hand. "Come on, Ascher, catch me." He touched his patch and threw the shoe overboard. Slats Shapiro and Barney Krinchuk raised their paddles toward the sky. Sig and me bent our heads and paddled. We finally reached the shore. We jumped out and turned the canoe around. I heard two or three Hiawathans cheer. Torpedo was already halfway across the lake. Ascher launched the Hawk and we climbed aboard. "Take off everything," he said, "everything." Me and Sig looked at him.

"Everything," Ascher said again. "The canoe's too heavy." And while me and Sig paddled, Ascher crawled across the canoe and took off our shirts, and our pants, and our shoes. He threw them overboard together with the bailing pot and started to undress. He took off his sneakers and his pants. "Ascher," I screamed, "the tattoos, the tattoos." He took off his shirt and flung it into the lake. All his cockamanies showed. Sig started to cry. "Now it's the Dungeon for us. For sure." Ascher swung his paddle. The sun shone all over him and for a second I thought that the Hirohitos and the Tojos on his chest were alive. We kept paddling. I shouted at the Judah. "Sink, bastard, sink." Call it magic or whatever you want, but a minute later I heard Slats Shapiro shout, "Torpedo, we're going down." Ascher jumped up near the bow of the Hawk. "Row, men, row." Sig started to cheer. "Chief," he said, "Chief, we're catching up." The Judah kept rocking from side to side. Water splashed over the gunwales. Torpedo ordered Slats and Barney to jump overboard. Ascher leaned over the side of the Hawk. "Try and ram me now, Torpedo." Slats and Barney swam toward the shore. Torpedo rowed with two paddles. We passed the Judah. "Drown, drown," Ascher said, swinging his paddle. The prow of the Judah began to tilt. All the Hiawathans crowded around the lakefront. Slats and Barney reached the shore. The Hiawathans booed and bombarded them with acorns. The Maccabees didn't even bother to protect them. They stood near the shore and watched Torpedo. Uncle Eddie held the trophy with his right hand, and with his left hand he scratched his ass. The Destroyer danced around Denny Lipshitz and played crazy songs on his bugle. "Ascher, Ascher, Ascher," all the Hiawathans cried. I turned around for a second. Torpedo's patch dropped down below his left eye. The eye was an empty pit. I didn't scream or anything when I saw it. The Judah kept sinking. Ascher poked me with his paddle. "Row," he said, "we didn't win yet." Sig sang the Hiawathan pep song. All the Hiawathans joined in. "Hiawatha, Hiawatha, 'ray, 'ray, 'ray." Even Ascher sang. Uncle Eddie shouted into the megaphone. "Torpedo, Torpedo, abandon your boat." I couldn't help it. I turned around again. The stern of the Judah was already under water. Only the tip of the bow showed. It wiggled back and forth. Torpedo kept paddling. Some water splashed into his empty eye. Uncle Eddie became a little frantic. "Torpedo, can you hear me? Abandon ship, abandon ship." Ascher poked me again. "Turn around, Dopey, and paddle. Turn around before I throw you overboard." He stood up near the bow and raised his arms. The Hiawathans pressed close to the shore and formed a chain. They surrounded Denny Lipshitz and Uncle Eddie, and shouted, "Ascher, Ascher, Ascher the Great." Ascher's body baked in the sun. Two Tojos and a Hitler showed through the wet cotton of his Fruit-of-the-Loom underpants. I heard something splash behind me. The bow and the stern of the Judah were raised above the water. No one was inside the canoe. Then I saw Torpedo's head surface near the Judah's stern. Torpedo was holding up the canoe, and his feet were kicking with the power of a six-cylinder engine. The Judah kept coming toward us. Sig's knees started to knock. "Chief," he said, "Chief, Torpedo's turned his canoe into a motorboat."

"Paddle!" Ascher said. He was ready to ram the Judah if it came too close. But Torpedo's feet couldn't match our paddles. We reached shore first. The Judah kept chugging. The Hiawathans surrounded the Hawk. I saw Torpedo close his empty eye just before little Wally Morgenthau and two other Hiawathans lifted me out of the canoe and carried me up the shore. The bow of the Judah struck a rock near the shore and the canoe spilled over. Torpedo stopped kicking. Barney Krinchuk led a few of the Maccabees toward the Judah. Slats Shapiro stayed by the shore. The Destroyer carried Ascher on his shoulders. Nobody said a word about the cockamanies. But Sig was still worried. "In two days the Destroyer will forget about the race, and then he'll remember the cockamanies. You'll see. It'll be the Dungeon for all of us." Little Wally Morgenthau told Sig to shut up.

Everybody could see that Uncle Eddie was happy. He wiggled his elephant-sized ass. Denny Lipshitz and two Maccabees carried Torpedo to the shore. Water was coming out of his nose and mouth, and his empty eye was leaking. The Hiawathans ignored him. Little Wally swiped Ascher's paddle and told everybody that he was going to put it in our trophy room. Uncle Eddie asked if Torpedo was all right. "Sure," Denny Lipshitz said. Slats Shapiro stood near the bow of the Hawk and cried. The Destroyer blew his bugle and Uncle Eddie and the Hiawathans walked toward Hiawatha House. Most of the parents followed them. I stayed behind.

Sing, Shaindele, Sing

At the Shamrock Gardens I was either Little Annie Rooney, the pride of Killarney, or Mary O'Reilly, the queen of County Cork. But at the Loew's Pitkin or the Henry Street Theatre I was Shaindele Berkowitz, the Molly Picon of East Broadway. In 1943 vaudeville was already on the way out, but my father could still count on a two-week stay at the Henry Street for the summer and winter reviews. After all, it was with "Shaindele" that I always scored my biggest successes. When I sang *Yussele* or *Oif'n Pripet-chik,* even the pennypinching furriers in the first row wept and threw dimes, and my father kept hopping across the stage and retrieved every cent. God help any of the stage

179

boys who tried to chisel my father out of a dime. He caught them after the show and taught them a lesson for life. My father paid Greenspan the tailor two dollars a week to teach me all the latest Jewish songs, and I spent night after night in the back of Greenspan's shop, singing and sipping tea with strawberry jam. His son Itzie was around most of the time, and he was always ready to pinch my behind or peek under my dress. But when his father caught him in the act, Itzie would throw up his hands and complain, "Pop, Pop, why should I want to start up with her? She's only a kid. Pop, the girl doesn't have a tit to her name." So I learned how to sing *Oif'n Pripetchik* like an expert, and had to put up with Itzie's antics. Greenspan showed me off to all his friends. "A goy," he would say, raising his right hand solemnly, "so help me God. A goy, but she's another Molly Picon. I should know. I taught her myself." I would have gladly performed for all of Greenspan's friends, but my father didn't allow me to give concerts for free.

My aunt Giuseppina sent the truant officers after me, but my father hopped from hotel to hotel so fast that no one could keep up with us. And once, after a session with Greenspan, I decided to visit my old neighborhood in the East Bronx. But as soon as I came near Webster Avenue Father Benjamini hailed me down. First he hugged me and asked me about my father, then his face darkened, and he told me that every soul in purgatory was wailing for me because of all the masses I had missed. "Fannie Finocchiaro," he said, "you're a lost soul." What could I tell him? What could I say? Call me Shaindele, Father. I'm the Molly Picon of East Broadway. So while he kept up his harangue, I ran off and promised myself that I would stay away from Webster Avenue for good.

I was fifteen in January, but my father still wouldn't let
me wear a brassière. "Fannie," he complained, "if they ever
find out you're over twelve, they'll banish us both." But even
my father couldn't hold back nature, and when I started to
grow in the right places he made me wear a towel around
my chest. So I remained flat-chested Fannie. And, God
forbid, if I ever went downstairs without the towel, he
pulled my hair and made me drink cod-liver oil for a week.
But we both knew that with or without the towel, my
vaudeville days were near the end of the line. The Shamrock
Gardens burned down in late '42, and the Loew's Pitkin
canceled its weekly vaudeville show. So in '43 we had to
settle for the Henry Street. I also sang at weddings and bar
mitzvahs, and we made enough to get by. And when Breitbart, the stage manager at the Henry Street, told my
father that he wanted Shaindele for the winter revue, I
was shipped back to Greenspan for more songs. Now Itzie
followed me around like a spider. After four or five sessions,
Greenspan told me that I was ready for the revue. "Fannie,"
he said, "Molly Picon better watch out. You'll drive all the
stars out of Second Avenue with your singing. I mean it." So
my father unpacked his accordion and we went over to
Henry Street.

In 1943 the Henry Street Theatre was already ancient.
Everyone waited for the theatre to close down. Half
the seats were broken, cockroaches and rats used the floor
for a playing field, and the curtains caught fire at least once
a month. Fire inspectors kept coming around and condemn-
ing the theatre, but Breitbart's brother knew the captain of
the Clinton Street precinct, and the theatre stayed open.
Breitbart's biggest problem was the balcony. It collapsed the
summer before, but Breitbart claimed that the Ludlow

Street Theatre hired some hooligans from Brownsville, and while Yankel the talking monkey was performing on stage, the hooligans brought hammers and hacksaws into the theatre and destroyed the balcony. Nobody knows if the story is true, but Breitbart sued the Ludlow Street Theatre for thousands, and even the police department was on his side. Breitbart himself installed two metal supports, but the balcony still kept rocking, and all the old-time actors bet that the balcony would collapse again, with or without the help of any hooligans.

So my father warned me, "Fannie, if you want to stay alive, don't stand under the balcony." And I took his advice. When Breitbart saw me, he called me over and started pinching my cheeks. "Shaindele," he said. My father stood in the corner and tuned up his accordion. Breitbart winked at me. "Shaindele, a cup of coffee after the show? Don't worry, I'll send your father on an errand." He winked again. Breitbart had a whole haremful of wives, daughters, and nieces, and he also had a double hernia and a punctured lung, but he still ran after all the girls in the show, and it didn't make any difference to him if they were twelve years old or sixty. "So, Shaindele?" he said, but he heard my father tuning up the accordion, and he stopped squeezing my behind. "Shaindele." The beams that supported the balcony began to shake. "Doomsday," my father said, and he dropped his accordion and hid behind one of the broken seats. I ran over to him. I heard him mumble a "Hail Mary" and promise Jesus that he would send me to St. Agnes' Secretarial School.

"Notte," Breitbart said, "come down from the balcony. Notte, move, before I skin you alive." A strange head peered over the balcony rail. Breitbart slapped his sides, com-

plained to me, and spoke to the wall, all at the same time.
"My nephew Notte. He's half an idiot, but what can I do?
He's part of the tribe. Give him a job, my wife tells me, give
him a job. But can he sweep the floor or draw a curtain?
No! Not Notte. All he can do is scribble poems that no one
can understand." My father stood up and went back to his
accordion. Breitbart's nephew Notte jumped over the rail-
ing, and climbed down one of the beams. The balcony
shook, but this time my father stood his ground. Notte's back
was slightly humped, his nose was crooked, several of his
teeth were missing, and he hardly had a chin. A pair of
stretched and worn suspenders supported his baggy pants.
He looked like a missing member of the Marx Brothers.
Breitbart rushed over to Notte and gripped his ears.
"This is what I pay you money for? To hide in balconies? My
philosopher! Every bone in your body I'll break. Nephew or
not!" My father laughed and worked the keys of his accordion with nimble fingers. Notte started to cough; his suspenders heaved and he had to hold up his baggy pants.
"Breitbart," I said, "leave him alone." Breitbart looked at me
and released Notte's ears. "Notte, look, you found yourself a
protector." Then he flung Notte halfway across the theatre.
"Pick up a broom. Sweep. Make a little trouble for the
cockroaches, or I'll send you packing without a dime. Nobody gets paid here for nothing." Notte picked up a broom.
Breitbart turned his back for a moment and shouted at the
stage boys. Notte's ears perked and one of his suspenders
popped, and I thought he was going to throw the broom at
Breitbart or leap across the theatre and pounce on him, but
he wiped his brow instead and smiled. He dropped the
broom and started to perform for me. He scowled and
mimicked Breitbart's motions. I laughed. Breitbart turned

around. He cursed Notte and chased after him. "A clown yet, a clown." Notte dodged between the seats. His baggy pants flopped and his unhooked suspender kept swinging back and forth. "Uncle, Uncle," he shouted, and then he ran behind the stage. I retrieved Notte's broom. My father came over to me and pinched my neck. "Fannie, you want to get us in trouble, huh? Don't interfere."

"What did I do, Papa, what did I do?" My father pushed me toward the stage. "Shut up and sing." I almost fell into the orchestra pit. My shoulder banged against an abandoned drum. I stood in front of the stage, and holding Notte's broom, I sang *Shain Vi Di Levone*. The stage boys stopped working and listened to me. Breitbart came over and congratulated me. "Shaindele," he said, "with you in the show, how can we lose?" Then he walked over to my father. I saw Notte standing behind the curtain. He smiled to me. I climbed up the steps of the stage. He took my hand and led me to one of the dressing rooms.

"Notte, why do you take such abuse?"

"Uncle's all right," Notte said. "He needs someone to knock around once in a while. It keeps him calm. And now I can afford my own room." He tugged his one workable suspender. "I'm a poet," he said, "and every poet needs a part-time job." He removed a crumpled cigarette from his pocket and broke it in half. Lumps of tobacco began to fall on his shoes. He stooped over, scooped together the shredded lumps, and stuffed them inside both cigarette halves. He straightened one of them and offered it to me. "Smoke, smoke," he said, "it's good for the brain." He lit both cigarettes. I coughed, and Notte patted my back. The tobacco was stale and tasted bitter, but I didn't want to disappoint Notte. So I smoked. He started pacing back and forth in the tiny room. "You'll see. One day Uncle will stage a play of mine, and then I'll be the one who gives out the orders. 'Uncle, raise the curtains. Uncle, add ten more seats. Uncle, put Mrs. Dushkin behind the pole. Her son crucified me yesterday in the *Forward.*'"

I laughed and almost swallowed the cigarette.

Notte kissed me. I kissed him back. We sat on the floor and Notte taught me how to play "show and tell."

He opened my blouse and saw the towel. "What's this? A new kind of underwear? *Vey iz mir!*"

"My father's orders," I said, and I took off the towel. Notte taught me another game.

I heard Breitbart and my father call me. "Shaindele."

"I'm telling you," Breitbart said, "she's with that monkey Notte."

I buttoned my blouse. Notte hid the towel in his pocket. We tiptoed out of the dressing room and went through a dark passageway. Notte held my hand. We came out near the other end of the stage. Notte draped the curtain around us and we kissed for the last time. I heard Breitbart and my father tramp across the passageway. "Notte," Breitbart shouted. Notte disappeared. My father saw me standing behind the curtain. He was ready to tear out my hair. Breitbart stopped him. "She's a valuable piece of property. You want to ruin the revue?" My father glared at me. He could see that I wasn't wearing the towel. "Where's Notte?" Breitbart said. "That's the question. *Notte.*" Notte's head appeared suddenly behind the balcony rail. "Uncle, I'm tracking down a cockroach."

Breitbart shook his fist at Notte and the balcony. "I'll beat you black and blue." Notte stood on the ledge of the balcony and laughed.

My father had rented a room at the Hotel Delancey, and when we came home he locked the door and went to work on me. He pulled my hair, twisted my nose, and wanted to know what had happened to the towel. I didn't tell him a thing. "Papa, no more towels. Either you let me wear a brassière, or I don't sing. That's final." He pulled my hair again, but he could see that I had already made up my mind. He took out a soiled handkerchief from the laundry bag and started to cry. "I'm a ruined man."

"Papa, no tricks. A brassière, papa, or you can kiss Shaindele goodbye."

So the next day I appeared at the theatre wearing my Maidenform. All the stage boys whistled. Breitbart looked at me and marveled. He clapped my father's back. "Congratulations. Berkowitz, the girl grew up overnight. Never mind the Molly Picon of East Broadway. Now we have the Lana Turner of Hester Street. Berkowitz, she'll be the star of the show. This I guarantee."

My father was a little overwhelmed. "Fannie," he whispered, "go out and buy a bigger size. We can't lose."

Only Notte seemed disappointed. "Show-off," he said.

"Notte," I told him, "if you want, I'll wear the towel again."

"The damage is done," he said, and picked up a broom.

Breitbart called me over. While my father's back was turned, he pinched both cups of the Maidenform. "Oy," he said, "I'll die. It's the real thing! Shaindele, Shaindele, meet me after the show." He took out his wallet. "Shaindele, a dress, a coat, a hat, whatever you want. It doesn't have to be Klein's. Let it be Saks or Gimpels. Buy, buy. What is money to me? Shaindele, is it a deal?"

"That's not in the contract."

His eyes closed. "Oy, and she's particular yet. That's what I like. A girl with spirit. Shaindele, refuse me all you want. It's good for the blood."

I walked away. I heard Notte mumbling to himself. "Nalewski Street, Niska Street, Muranow Square . . ."

"Notte," I said, "what are you doing?—going on a tour of Brooklyn? There's no Niska Street in the Bronx. Notte, where is—"

"In *Warsaw*," Notte said, "where else! Jews are dying all over the world, and I'm stuck here. Uncle is right. A fool, a dope, a clown, this is what I am."

"Notte, I thought you wanted to be a poet."

His lips twisted grimly. "A machine gun in the right hands is also poetry."

"Notte, if you want to fight, join up with the army or the marines. My Uncle Dom is a captain already."

"Who would take me?—I'm sixteen." He raised his shoulder. "And a cripple to the bargain! And suppose they took me, where would they send me?—to fight the Japs. Better I'll stay here and collect *zlotys* for the resistance. Later I'll join the Jewish Commandos in Tel Aviv, and then we'll all parachute over Niska Street, and send the Germans to Gehenna."

Breitbart saw us standing together. "Notte, make an appointment with the broom before I hang you from the ceiling. Shaindele, it's time to sing."

That evening I asked my father for two dollars.

"Papa," I said, "a girl that wears a brassière has to have an allowance."

He pulled my hair for five minutes and gave me fifty cents.

The next day I saw Notte standing under the balcony and gave him the fifty cents. "For the resistance," I said. "That's all I could raise." His ears shone. "Shaindele," he said. Breitbart was standing behind us. "Later, in back of the stage."

So I sang three songs for Breitbart and the stage boys and met Notte in the dressing room. We didn't waste any time. Notte gave me a marathon kiss, but he boycotted my brassière. He refused to let me unhook it. Notte taught me a few more games, and I kept my brassière on. Then he pinned a cardboard medal on me, and congratulated me. I was now a Jewish Commando. We kissed some more, and he handed me a sheet of paper. I was a little baffled. "A poem," he said.

"Notte, I'm not a dope. I know." The poem was in Jewish. "Notte," I said, "read it to me. I can't see so good without my glasses."

Notte read the poem. I didn't understand a word, but I cried anyway. I'm sure it was a beautiful poem. I heard Breitbart call me. "Tomorrow," Notte said, "same time, same place." He disappeared before I could kiss him, or thank him, or anything.

Greenspan came over to the theatre the day before the opening of the show. He wanted to see his prodigy. He brought Itzie with him. When Itzie saw me with my Maidenform on, he ran over with his hands outstretched.

"Fannie." Notte held him off. He had a broom in one hand and a hammer in the other. "Fannie," Itzie said, "call off the hatchetman. I'll break him in twenty pieces. I mean it." Notte raised the hammer.

"You I'll fix," Itzie said, but he walked away.

"Shaindele, who, who is Fannie?"

"Notte, that's my nickname in the Bronx."

Itzie left the theatre. Greenspan came over. He stared at my Maidenform. "*Mazel tov!*" He clapped his hands twice. "Shaindele, sing. Sing for me, Shaindele, sing." So I sang the whole afternoon. Greenspan kept kissing me. Breitbart called me over a dozen times and made more proposals. "Shaindele, a Persian-lamb coat, a room at the Waldorf, anything you want. Name it and it's yours."

Itzie came back with two of his friends. They were carrying something under their coats. I saw Notte walk behind the stage. Itzie and his friends followed him. "Shaindele," Breitbart said, "if you don't trust me, I'll bring over my lawyer. We'll sign an agreement. Shaindele, you want the theatre? Take it, it's yours!"

"Later, Breitbart, later." I ran behind the stage. Itzie and his friends were in the dressing room. Notte was sitting on the floor. His nose was bleeding, and his forehead was bruised. Itzie's friends were holding baseball bats. "Notte, what did they do to you, Notte?" Itzie locked the door. "Okay, Fannie," he said, "now we'll find out what you're worth. And if you make one sound, your friend gets a dented head for himself." Itzie's friends brandished the bats over Notte's head. They found some rope and tied Notte to a chair. Then they held my arms, and Itzie tore off my Maidenform and everything else. They wound the brassière around

Notte's head. And they made Notte watch. I cried the whole time. Itzie's friends picked up the baseball bats and then they left. I untied Notte. His body was shaking. I kissed his nose, his forehead, and his eyes. We left the dressing room.

I told my father that I didn't want to sing. "Fannie," he said, "you'll ruin me for life. Breitbart can throw me in jail. And believe me, he will. What happened to your brassière?"

"I threw it away."

My father slapped his sides. "The girl is an idiot. Notte number two!"

He went down on his knees. "Fannie, it's the poorhouse for me."

I finally agreed to sing. "Remember, Papa, after this, no more shows."

He kissed my hands. "Papa," I said, "get off the floor."

The theatre was packed. Every seat in the orchestra and balcony was taken, and Breitbart gave out cushions to all the latecomers and told them to sit on the floor. "I never saw such a house," Breitbart said. "It's better than before the war. Even Michelesko never drew such a crowd." But when Breitbart saw me without my Maidenform, he became furious. "What's the gimmick, Berkowitz?"

"The girl's depressed," my father said. "She'll be all right by tomorrow. You'll see."

"I'm not worried about tomorrow. It's today what's on my mind. You see them out there. You want them to tear up the place?" Breitbart sent home one of the stage boys to borrow a brassière from his wife. The boy came back with a brassière that was three sizes too big. But I had to put it on. "That's better," Breitbart said. "No more gimmicks."

Yankel the talking monkey went on stage first. With the

help of Rosenblum the ventriloquist, Yankel told dirty
stories in Jewish, Polish, Russian, and Roumanian, but the
crowd was bored. I could hear the men and women in the
first row stamp their feet and shout, "Shaindele, Shaindele."
Breitbart called Yankel off the stage. "Enough, Rosenblum,
before they tear off the seats and throw them at you.
Enough." Next Minna Mendelsohn sang *Der Rebbe Eli
Melech,* and her husband Boris leaned one knee over a
chair and strummed his balalaika. I opened the curtain an
inch and looked out. I cupped my hands over my eyes and
saw Itzie sitting in the first row of the balcony. This time he
had nine or ten friends with him. They were stamping their
feet and shouting, "Sing, Shaindele, sing." My Notte was
standing near the orchestra pit. Breitbart pushed me away
from the curtain. "You want to spoil the show? Nobody is
allowed to see you before you go out on stage." Everybody
kept hooting and stamping their feet. "Sing, Shaindele, sing."
Minna Mendelsohn never finished her song. Someone
climbed up on the stage, stole her husband's chair, and flung
it into the orchestra pit. "Cancel all the other acts," Breitbart
said. "Bring out Shaindele." My father's knees were knocking. "Berkowitz, you want to get us all killed? Pick up your
accordion and let's go." Everybody stood up and cheered
when they saw me. My father brought out his accordion,
and someone booed. He ran behind the curtain. "Breitbart,
please," I heard my father scream. "They don't want me.
They want Shaindele." Breitbart cursed him and let him stay
behind the curtain. The stage lights blinded me for a moment, but after a while I became used to them. A man in the
second row started to dance across the aisle. He must have
been about seventy years old. *"Mommenu,"* he said, "look at

the tits on her! Better than a seven-course meal." Everybody
sitting next to him started to laugh. I heard Itzie shout,
"Sing, Shaindele, sing." Notte was still standing near the
orchestra pit. He saw that my hands were shaking, and he
smiled for the first time. "Notte," I said, and I started to sing.
I didn't sing for Breitbart, or Itzie, or my father, or anybody
in the second row, I sang only for Notte. *Yussele, Shain Vi
Di Levone, Oif'n Pripetchik, Gai Ich Mir Shpatzieren,
Ot Azoy Nait A Shneider,* all for Notte. The man in the
second row clapped his hands. "Never mind the *titzgehs.*
The girl has a *goldene shtimme.* Sing, Shaindele, sing." They
wouldn't let me off the stage. Itzie and his friends kept
stamping their feet. I sang *Yussele* for the fifth time. The
beams that held up the balcony began to shake. First there
was a rumbling sound. Breitbart peered through the curtain.
"Stop the show." I heard a woman scream. Then the balcony
came tumbling down.

We stayed in the hotel for two days. My father wouldn't
let me see Notte or anybody. He kept making phone calls.
"Fannie, pack your underwear. We're going to Chicago.
Who needs trouble? If anybody finds out that we were
associated with the Henry Street Theatre we're finished.
Breitbart is in jail. Even his father-in-law is suing him. He
was sitting in the balcony. Fannie, pack, pack."

I refused.

He rocked his head back and forth. "Fannie, they're opening up a theatre on Maxwell Street in Chicago. They want
an accordion player. You won't even have to sing. We'll be
back in two, three weeks."

"I don't go before I say goodbye to Notte."

"Go, but put on some kind of disguise. If they catch you in the street they'll burn you alive."

I wore a kerchief and one of my father's old coats, and I went looking for Notte. The Henry Street Theatre was boarded up, and I couldn't get inside. I called up Breitbart's home, but no one answered. I went to the Clinton Street precinct. Then I tried all the rooming houses. "Notte," I said, "Notte." I didn't even know his last name. I came back to the hotel without finding Notte. We left for Chicago the next day.

There were no theatres on Maxwell Street, only meat markets. My father apologized. "Fannie, I was desperate. We had to get out." He became a butcher and worked in a kosher meat market. In April I heard about the uprising in the Warsaw ghetto. "Niska Street," I said to myself. I still had my Jewish Commando badge. I wrote over a hundred letters to Notte. They all said the same thing: "Notte, please come and get me. I live on Maxwell Street over the Morgenstern Meat Market." I mailed ten of the letters to Breitbart, a few to the Henry Street Theatre, one to the Clinton Street precinct, one to the Hotel Delancey, one to Greenspan, and the rest to people I knew who lived near Delancey Street. Most of the letters came back. I put on different envelopes, and sent them out again. But Notte never showed up.

Format by Morris Karol
Set in Lintoype Caledonia
Composed, printed and bound by American Book–Stratford Press
HARPER & ROW, PUBLISHERS, INCORPORATED